Memory House

On the far edge of Richmond, Virginia, there is a section called Burnsville. It's a little-known patch of winding streets and quaint houses, some of which date back to the nineteenth century. Ophelia Browne lives in the white house at the end of Haber Street.

A passerby would not readily notice her house. It is small and simple, partially hidden by a weeping willow older than the house itself. In the sunlit room that was once her front parlor, Ophelia now has a small apothecary shop. The shelves are lined with bottles and baskets of powders and potions that can produce beauty in the eye of the beholder, cure hiccups, restore faith and some say even cause an impossible love to blossom.

Beyond the shop a narrow hallway leads to two bedrooms at the back of the house. These are the rooms Ophelia rents to weary souls who come in search of a night's rest.

Only those with a sharp eye will see the tiny sign planted alongside the walkway, and only those in need of solace will pull to the side of the street, park partway on the grass and rap the brass knocker on the front door.

⚬━◆━⚬

When Annie Cross leaves Philadelphia she has no destination in mind. She simply wants to get away from Michael, to get away from a thousand subtle reminders of the love that has died a slow and painful death. For years they'd been good together; then something happened.

Not one big argument; just a long stretched-out series of small slights and pointy barbs. In the end he'd moved out, taking his stuff and leaving behind a note that claimed he was sorry.

The truth is Annie was as weary of the relationship as Michael, and had she been the one to leave it might not have pained her heart as it did. But she wasn't the one to leave. He was. He moved on and found himself a new apartment, one without stale memories and bitterness clinging to the walls. She was left behind, stuck in their old life but with a chunk of it missing.

Michael is gone and yet he isn't. There is the razor he left on the bathroom shelf, the slippers still tucked under his side of the bed and the smell of musky cologne that lingers in the half-empty closet. Magazines addressed to Michael Stavros still cram the mailbox, and the doormen still greet her as Missus Stavros.

The irony of it was that they weren't married. They never had been. In the beginning it was what they'd fought about most often, but in time that issue grew thin and morphed itself into countless smaller and less significant problems—a toilet seat left up, newspapers scattered across around the living room, a burnt pork chop, an unwashed coffee pot. Their complaints became unvoiced words, like bricks of resentment and anger stacked on both sides of an invisible wall.

Weekdays Annie can lose herself in work. She can dash out the door, grab a coffee at Starbucks and get through the day without reminders. But the evenings are long and weekends torturous.

She and Michael had been together for seven years, and in those years her friends got married and started raising families. Occasionally two or three couples got together for an evening out, but it was always couples and the conversation was most often about children and home repairs. Neither subject interested Michael, and he made no effort to hide his feelings. Little by little her friends fell away, and now Annie is left with a handful of colleagues at the office and a few neighbors living on the fifth floor of the Remington Arms.

That Friday afternoon when Annie tosses her overnight bag into the back seat of the Toyota and pulls out of the garage she is hoping to forget. Little does she know this trip will be the start of remembering.

⌇

Annie almost misses the sign, hidden as it is behind the swaying branches of the weeping willow. She stops the car and peers down the dimly lit walkway. A split second before she is ready to shift into drive and move on, the last ray of sunlight dances across the gold lettering and she sees the words "Memory House Bed & Breakfast." Years earlier the sign was white as fresh-fallen snow, but over time it has aged to a color that is now all but invisible against the dusk of evening. Only the gold lettering remains as bright as it has always been.

Annie parks the car, straddling the gully between the street and the grass. She hoists her overnight bag from the back seat and starts up the walkway. A few steps from the front porch she feels a tingle at the back of her neck, and suddenly it seems she's been here before. A feeling of familiarity settles over her, and for a fleeting moment she hears the whisper of words. Startled, she stops and turns. She expects to see someone following in her footsteps, but there is only a small splatter of sunlight and the fluttering branches of the willow.

Glancing over her shoulder once more, she steps onto the porch and raps the knocker. When the door creaks open, a little old lady stands in the glow of yellow lamplight.

"Good evening," Ophelia Browne says.

Annie hesitates for a moment then replies, "The fellow down at the gas station suggested your place for a bed and breakfast. I don't have a reservation but I thought maybe…"

Ophelia can see the weary look on the girl's face. "No need to apologize. I've got no other guests tonight, so there's plenty of room."

Annie smiles, introduces herself and then follows the woman into the center hall. As they walk toward the back rooms, Annie catches the scent of something sweet—roses maybe or gardenias. It would be two, possibly three months before such flowers would bloom in Philadelphia, but she'd traveled south so conceivably…

"Is that roses I smell?" she asks.

Ophelia gives a soft chuckle. "No, that's my potpourri." She points a gnarled finger toward the glass bowl sitting atop a tiny three-legged table.

"Oh." Annie nods. "Made from dried roses?"

Ophelia shakes her head. "No roses. It's mostly passion flower and vanilla."

Annie takes a deep breath. "Funny, I don't smell vanilla at all."

"You wouldn't unless vanilla was your favorite fragrance. It's a remembrance blend. It reminds you of something that's brought happiness."

Annie stops, turns back and sniffs the air again. This time she catches the scent of lilacs. It is so powerful that if she closes her eyes she will imagine herself a child again, still living in the house where the fragrance of summertime lilacs drifted through her bedroom window.

The thought of a potpourri that changes scent teases Annie's mind. As she follows Ophelia down the hallway she asks, "Would it smell like chicken soup to someone who has good memories of chicken soup?"

Ophelia nods.

"What about burnt toast?"

Ophelia chuckles aloud. "I can't imagine burnt toast being someone's favorite, but, yes, it would give off the smell of burnt toast." She stops and eases the door on the right side of the hallway open. "Here's your room."

The room is decorated in pinks and mauves; it has the look of a little girl's room, a bouquet of prints blending into one another and the large double bed covered in a comforter that appears fluffy as a cloud.

"It's lovely," Annie exclaims. She steps inside and sets her overnight case down alongside a large mahogany dresser.

Ophelia makes no attempt to close the door, nor does she walk away.

She watches Annie move around the room, first touching her hand to one thing and then another: the crocheted doily on the dresser, the ruffled curtain, a silk lampshade.

"This is my favorite room," Ophelia says. "It overlooks a pond filled with ducks and geese. The squawking can be a bit annoying early in the morning, but they are a delight to watch. If you think the noise will bother you—"

"Not at all," Annie replies. "I'm an early riser."

"Well, then, I'll leave you to settle in." Ophelia pulls the door closed and starts back down the hall. She's gone only a scant two or three steps when a thought comes to her and she turns back.

She raps on the bedroom door and calls out, "Excuse me." When the door swings open she says, "It occurred to me that you might not have had dinner."

Annie smiles. "Actually I haven't. Maybe you could suggest a nearby place—"

"I've made a wonderful stew," Ophelia interrupts her. "I'd love to have you share it with me."

"If you're sure it's no trouble."

"No trouble at all," Ophelia replies. "Get yourself settled then come around to the kitchen." She turns and walks off.

Annie cannot see the smile that curls the old woman's lips.

A PINCH OF ROSEMARY

Ophelia Browne remembers everything. She remembers things from her own life and from the lives of those who came before her. She has only to touch her hand to an object and she can feel the special memory clinging to it. But now she is getting on in years. In eleven months she'll turn ninety. Few women in the Browne family live beyond such an age. If death comes before she finds a replacement, the memories might be lost forever. Ophelia prays this won't happen.

For the past five years she's studied the face of every guest arriving on her doorstep. She's looked into their eyes and seen the souls of people rooted to reality. Not one has shown even a flicker of promise, and time is growing short.

Now there is hope. This new guest, the girl from Pennsylvania, could easily be the one. Ophelia noticed it the moment she opened the door. The girl has the look of a person who can see beyond what is and reach back for what was. Seldom has Ophelia come across such deep violet eyes and never with the flecks of green that once danced in her own reflection.

With the passing of time, the color of Ophelia's eyes has changed. They are now a steely gray but in her younger years they were violet, the same deep shade as those of the girl.

A broad smile spreads across the old woman's face as she reaches into the kitchen cupboard and pulls a never-before-used jar from the top shelf. She pries open the top, sprinkles a generous helping of the dried leaves into the stew and begins to stir.

When Annie walks into the kitchen the stew is simmering on the stove, and the table is set with white porcelain dishes and silver spoons. In the center of the table is a basket piled high with biscuits.

"Oh my goodness," Annie exclaims, "everything smells so delicious." She glances around to make sure it is not another scent-switching potpourri tickling her senses.

"It's the biscuits," Ophelia replies. "Nothing smells as good as biscuits fresh from the oven." She motions to the chair on the far side of the table, invites Annie to sit and then asks if she would care for something to drink.

The day has been long and tiring. Highways with little to look at. Billboards touting burgers and outlet malls. Tractor-trailers rumbling by. Bugs splattering across the windshield. Annie would like something to ease the tension in her shoulders and the stiffness in her back. She thinks of a glass of burgundy but before she can mention it, Ophelia suggests, "Dandelion tea, perhaps?"

A bit disappointed with the alternative, Annie curls her mouth into a shallow smile.

"I've never had dandelion tea," she says, "but I'd be willing to try it."

Ophelia pours two cups of tea, then settles herself in the other chair.

At first the tea seems to have a slightly bitter tang, but after only a few sips Annie discovers it has a sweetness that lingers on her tongue. She helps herself to a biscuit, butters it lavishly and continues sipping the tea. By time the cup is empty the tension in her shoulders is gone, and she's completely forgotten the stiffness in her back. She's also forgotten about Michael.

Seeing the relaxed smile on the girl's face, Ophelia says, "The stew should be done by now." She rises from her chair, stirs the mixture once more time and then fills both bowls.

After a single mouthful Annie declares the stew delicious. "Is this lamb I taste?"

"Afraid not." Ophelia laughs. "It's the herbs and vegetables from my garden."

Annie looks up wide-eyed. With her spoon stalled halfway to her mouth, she gasps. "You have a garden?"

"Of course. Why wouldn't I?"

Struggling with such a thought, Annie says, "But isn't it rather strenuous for a woman your age? Bending down, digging in the dirt?"

"I'm a Browne," Ophelia replies. "Brownes are made of sturdy stock."

"I suppose so." Annie lowers the spoonful of stew back into the bowl and sits quietly. How could it be, she wonders, that a woman so far along in years does all this and she, a person who is not yet thirty-three, does nothing? Perhaps if she'd been born a Browne...

For a brief span of time both women are caught up in their own thoughts of what was and what could have been.

Ophelia, wrapped in the pleasantries of memory, begins telling how as a toddler she'd learned to love growing things. She goes on for almost ten minutes describing the trailing vines of nasturtium, patches of crimson clover and rows of basil growing side by side with thyme.

"And then there's rosemary," she says. "Add the tiniest pinch of that to your tea, and you're certain to have sweet dreams."

Annie has not enjoyed pleasant dreams for a good number of years. They would certainly be a welcome change from the restless nights of wondering what had gone wrong.

"Is there any rosemary in this tea?" she asks hopefully.

A faraway look shadows Ophelia's face as she shakes her head. "No. This is dandelion tea. I drink it because..."

She stops, knowing it is too soon to speak of the gift. After a few seconds of hesitation, she moves on to telling how ginger can produce a heated love affair.

As she explains how eucalyptus leaves can be ground into a powder that will cure even the common cold, Ophelia notices the girl's expression grow somber.

"Have I said something wrong?" she asks.

Annie sighs. "Not at all. I'm just a bit envious."

"Envious of an old lady?"

Annie gives a tight little laugh. "Not really. But I do envy your ability to grow such wonderful things."

"Shoot, anybody can garden. It doesn't take a whole lot of know-how. You drop the seeds in the ground and then—" Ophelia is going to say God does the rest, but she never gets the chance.

"Ground." Annie grimaces. "That's the problem. I live on the fifth floor of an apartment building. There's no place to plant anything. Once in a while a blade of grass pops up between the bricks in the courtyard, but that's it."

Ophelia nods knowingly. "I see what you mean."

For several minutes they sit quietly, each waiting for the other to speak. If you were to look inside the two minds you could see they wanted the same thing, but there is no obvious way of getting to it. When the silence grows thick as fog, they both open their mouths at the very same moment.

"I was thinking—"

"If you wouldn't mind—"

The words bump into each other, and they begin to laugh.

Annie spreads her hands with palms up. "You first."

"Okay." Ophelia laughs. "I was thinking if you're going to be here a few days, you could try your hand in my garden."

Annie's fingers fly to her mouth and she guffaws aloud. "That's the craziest thing ever!"

"It's not that crazy," Ophelia says. "I only offered because—"

Annie stops her. "I didn't mean the idea was crazy, I meant it was crazy because I was going to say if you wouldn't mind maybe I could help out in your garden."

They laugh again, and the jumble of words evolves into a conversation of possibilities. Ophelia promises to show the girl a world of wonders, a world of growing things and potions that can repair even a broken heart. Annie's eyes glow an even deeper shade of violet with the tiny green flickers sparkling as she listens.

And thus it is decided. Although she has brought only enough clothes for a three-day getaway, Annie now plans to stay the week. She will rinse out her undies each night and make do with the single pair of jeans she's packed. Any other time such a change of plans would be unthinkable, but this time it is different. Like Alice falling down the rabbit hole, she is caught up in a magical adventure.

They sit and talk as the evening sky turns black and thunder sounds in the distance. When the grandfather clock chimes twelve, Ophelia sets the teakettle on to boil. It has become her custom each night to savor a cup of the special tea before retiring. Filling the diffuser with crushed leaves, she brews a mug of dandelion tea for herself. For Annie, who will soon enough come to know the power of the special tea, she creates a steaming mix of lavender and rosemary.

As the girl wraps her fingers around the warm mug and sips the fragrant mix she sighs. "I'm so lucky to have found the Memory House. It's almost a miracle."

"Indeed it is." Ophelia touches her bony fingers to the girl's shoulder and smiles. "Indeed it is."

By the time the mugs are empty, Annie has begun to yawn.

"Oh my gosh," she says, "I can hardly keep my eyes open."

"It's late," Ophelia says. "Go to bed; get some sleep."

Annie yawns again. "I'll stay and help you clean up," she offers, but as she stands her eyelids begin to droop.

"Nonsense," Ophelia says. "There's nothing but two mugs to rinse. Now shoo on out of here and get to bed."

Growing sleepier by the second Annie answers, "Okay."

Once back in the cozy room, she slides beneath the comforter and is lost to sleep in mere seconds.

After Ophelia snaps the kitchen light off, she walks to the back hall and listens for sounds of sleep from the girl's room. In the still of night she can hear most anything—grass growing, a cloud moving and, yes, even the sound of her new guest dreaming. Once she hears the soft whisper of sleep she turns and starts toward the staircase.

She takes the stairs one at a time, slowly moving up and onto each step, first with her right leg, then bringing up the left. It is an arduous task because of the arthritis in her left knee, but Ophelia is not ready to abandon the loft. It is where she stores her finest treasures. It is closer to heaven, and it's where memories are the sweetest.

It matters not that the oak boards of the floor are rough in spots and the whitewash of the walls has now faded into nothingness. The loft is a place where she can close her eyes and memories come without bidding. On a warm summer night when the windows are open and sounds float on a breeze, she can touch her hand to the Bible or the snow globe and hear the voices of children playing in the yard. How sweet they are. How young and unsuspecting.

On this night when Ophelia closes her eyes, the memories are sparse and she wonders if the time has come for her to leave the house. Although such a thought crosses her mind, she knows she will never do it. There is nowhere on earth like this house. It is tucked into the back corner of a lot that overlooks the pond where ducks and geese come summer after summer. The neighbors claim the birds settle in this pond because it is sheltered and the water remains warm until late November.

But Ophelia knows the real reason they return. They come back because this is a place meant for remembering.

OPHELIA BROWNE

I came to this house seventy years ago when Edward and I were newly married. He'd just passed his twenty-third birthday and I was not yet twenty. Oh, how in love we were. I thought surely no woman ever loved a man as much as I loved Edward. Just looking at him made my insides feel warm.

With Edward by my side, ordinary things became special—the sunrise came in a burst of optimism and color, the rain against the window took on the sound of a song, even lingering in bed a few moments longer on wintery mornings was reason to celebrate.

Before we happened upon this place we were happy living in our rented apartment, but once we'd seen the house everything changed. There is a certain magic here; we both felt it the minute we stepped across the threshold. "This is where you belong," Edward whispered in my ear, and I nodded happily.

We scraped together enough for a down payment, and within the month we moved in. We didn't have money for furniture but we didn't care. On warm summer nights we'd take a blanket out to the yard and lie side by side in the grass. We'd stay there for hours, looking up at the stars and talking about all the things we were going to do.

Ah, what wonderful dreams we had. He promised that one day we would see Paris, visit the pyramids and toss coins into the Fountain of Trevi. There were times when I would rest my head in his lap and close my eyes as he spoke of how we'd stroll through the shops then stop at a patisserie for a warm croissant and cup of hot chocolate. Listening to Edward tell of it, I felt like we were already there.

Lord God, those were happy days. That kind of happiness is something that needs to be remembered. If you start forgetting, it dies and you're left with just the misery of what is instead of the joy of what was.

I wallowed in such misery for almost two years; then Edward told me to start remembering the good times and close out the tragedy that came after them. It's not your fault, he said, and smiled with those blue eyes of his sparkling like stars. I heard his voice clear as a bell, but the moment I reached out for him he vanished into thin air. For weeks I wondered if it was the sadness making me crazy. But when I got to thinking that, I'd go back to the loft. Up there things made more sense and good memories came easier.

Some people are afraid of dying but not me. I know when I get to heaven I'll find my dear sweet Edward again. He'll pull me in into his arms and start telling me of all the places we can float off to.

How can you be afraid of something as wonderful as that?

THE GARDEN

Saturday morning Annie wakes with a smile on her face. For several minutes she remains in bed savoring the sweetness of a dream that has now left her. She remembers only a feeling of happiness but cannot remember the dream itself. It was not of Michael, that she knows. Thoughts of him have almost vanished, and the emptiness of the hole he left behind has somehow been filled. There is a strange new excitement pulsing through her veins, an excitement she hasn't felt in a very long time.

She tosses the coverlet back, climbs from the bed and pulls on her jeans. This sudden interest in growing things is an odd turn of events, but she is not in the mood to question it. She is ready for change, ready for something new, ready to leave her worn and weary thoughts behind.

Breezing into the kitchen, she sees Ophelia already at the stove. "Good morning," she says brightly.

Ophelia returns the smile and motions Annie to sit. "I know you enjoyed these yesterday." She sets a basket of biscuits and a jar on honey on the table. The yeasty aroma is as enticing as it was last night.

This time Annie does not hesitate. She helps herself to a biscuit and spreads it with honey that is thick with pieces of honeycomb.

"This isn't from the store, is it?" she asks. Her words sound garbled coming through a mouthful of warm sweetness, but Ophelia understands.

"No, it isn't," she answers. "I keep a hive at the far end of the garden."

Annie chuckles. "Is there anything you can't do?"

"Oh, there are many things I can't do," Ophelia replies. "But I try not to think of them. Such thoughts only weigh a person down."

Annie is still pondering the truth of that when Ophelia sets a platter of pancakes and bacon on the table, then pours two cups of dandelion tea.

Annie is a coffee-drinker and finds it almost impossible to start the day without a full mug. But on this particular morning she sips the dandelion tea and says nothing. Although it is pale in color and thin compared to the robust coffee she drinks, it is strangely satisfying. The bitterness that first stung her tongue is gone; in its place is a sweet aftertaste that reminds her of cherry wine.

Once the breakfast dishes are dried and put away, Ophelia leads Annie through a mudroom where she stops to put on a large straw hat. She hands a second one to Annie. It looks newer, not yet bleached by the sun. Together they go out the side door and into a garden larger than Annie imagined it might be.

The house is set back from the street so far that newcomers expect no backyard, which is almost true. The edge of the pond is a scant ten or fifteen feet from the back door. There is only a narrow strip of grass in the back, but on the far side of the house is a field wider perhaps than the house itself. Angled back behind the large willow, the garden is impossible to see from the street.

Annie gasps. "You planted this yourself?"

Ophelia nods with a proud smile. She then confesses that Tom, a farmer from the next town, turned the soil.

"That's the hard part," she says, "but he's willing to do it in exchange for a basket of potpourri."

They walk toward the rows of plants, and Ophelia stops at the tool shed to pull out a small ladder-back chair with sawed off legs. She hands it to Annie.

"Can you carry this?" she asks. Then she turns back to pick up the basket of gardening tools she hooks over her own arm.

When they reach the spot where a patch of yellow blossoms is taller than Ophelia's knee, she takes the chair from Annie and sits in it. As she snips the heads of flowering yarrow they talk.

"What brought you to Memory House?" Ophelia asks.

Annie hesitates a moment, shrugs, then gives a lighthearted laugh. "Fate, I guess. I'm awfully glad to be here, but I think my finding this place was just pure luck."

Ophelia smiles as Annie continues, telling of how she simply wanted to get away from the bad memories Michael left behind. Although the girl doesn't realize it, she has answered Ophelia's question.

Ophelia tends the garden every day, but it is not the rows of plantains and rosemary that keep her at the house; it is the memories. She fears her treasures will lose their power if taken away from here. This is where it began, and Ophelia believes this is where it must stay.

❦

After spending the morning in the garden they return to the house. Ophelia leaves her dirty shoes in the mudroom and slides her feet into the slippers she keeps beneath the counter. Annie removes her sneakers and follows along barefoot. They go into the apothecary shop where Ophelia will hang some of the herbs and flowers she has gathered to dry. It will take days, maybe weeks, but in time they will be ready.

The apothecary shop is a small room with two silk chairs and a cluster of small tables. On each of the tables there is a display of Ophelia's wares. One table has a basket with a perfusion of different-colored rose petals. Another has a potpourri with the smell of gingerbread cookies. A long table serves as a counter, and the wall behind it is lined with shelves. They contain bottles, jars and tins labeled with words Annie has never seen before.

"What's Mugwort?" she asks.

Ophelia laughs. "It's just an herb," she answers and continues arranging the last of the day's cuttings on a drying rack.

Annie traces her finger, along the other tins: damiana, Queen Elizabeth, orris, archangel.

"Don't tell me you actually have an archangel bottled up in this jar," she quips.

"Archangel is a root," Ophelia answers. "When ground into powder and sewn into a sachet, it's believed to protect children."

Annie turns with a look of skepticism stretched across her face. "Really?"

Ophelia nods as she slides the last drying tray into place. "I grew up in the mountains of West Virginia where most believed in the healing power of herbs and roots. Perhaps it's just an old wives' tale, perhaps not." She turns, leans closer to Annie and in a voice almost a whisper says, "But I can say for sure, when a new mama stitches an archangel sachet into her baby's pillow, that woman's heart rests easier."

With her work in the apothecary now finished, Ophelia suggests they freshen up and have lunch on the side porch.

Although it takes Annie just a short while to wash up and change into the gabardine slacks she wore yesterday, when she gets to the porch a tray of sandwiches is already sitting on the table. Skirted with a cloth that puddles on the floor, the table is set with Limoges porcelain dishes.

Moments later Ophelia appears with a tray of iced tea and cookies.

"Here, let me help you with that." Annie takes the tray and sets it on the table. "You shouldn't have gone to all this trouble."

Ophelia claims it is no trouble, and this is true. These are the things she enjoys doing. An elegant lunch on the side porch reminds her of Edward. It is as it was back then, when he sat across from her. She reaches for the small bouquet of roses on the teacart, and when her hand touches the vase she can hear Edward's voice. It is a sound she has lived with all these years. A sound that is both sweet and sorrowful.

Ophelia has finished her sandwich and is nibbling on an almond cookie when the clang of a cowbell sounds. "A customer," she explains and pushes back from the table.

"May I tag along?" Annie asks. The apothecary intrigues her.

With the girl trailing her, Ophelia enters the shop and gives a warmhearted greeting to the middle-aged man she calls Sam. Although he is pot-bellied and balding, he has a smile that is almost infectious.

"What are you in need of today?" Ophelia asks.

Sam hesitates a moment, looks over at Annie then motions toward the far corner of the room. When he walks over there, Ophelia follows.

"I ain't comfortable talking in front of strangers," he whispers.

Instead of explaining Annie, Ophelia simply gives a knowing nod and listens. The truth is the shop is so small even the tiniest whisper can be heard, no matter where a person stands.

"I've got Eloise Green coming for dinner tonight," Sam says, "and I'm planning to ask if she'll marry me. You got something that will…?"

Ophelia leans in acting every bit as secretive as Sam. "I certainly do," she whispers. Promising the preparation will be ready in a minute, she takes a small dish from the shelf and mixes a thimbleful of damiana with a like amount of crushed lavender buds, then adds a pinch of thyme. She pours the mixture into a small bottle and hands it to Sam.

"A word of advice," she tells him. "This works better when it is sprinkled over a round of roast beef."

Sam smiles. "That's sure enough what I'm gonna do." He hands Ophelia a folded-up dollar bill and leaves the shop whistling.

When he is beyond earshot Annie asks, "Is that true?"

Ophelia laughs. "True enough. Roast beef is Eloise's favorite food, and the mixture I gave Sam will make the meat even more flavorful."

"But what if she doesn't love him? Or doesn't want to get married?"

With a sly little grin curling the corners of her mouth, Ophelia answers, "Eloise was in here two weeks ago and got a bottle of rosewater cologne. She asked if rosewater could encourage a man like Sam to propose."

"But…" Annie stuttered, "if you knew they wanted to marry one another…"

"I knew, but they didn't know. Things like rosewater and damiana won't make a person fall in love, but thinking it will can give them the courage they need to make it happen."

Ophelia bends and pulls a small wooden box from the bottom shelf. "Besides, it's for a good cause. The money I make in the store goes to the Sisters of Mercy."

Lifting the lid of the box, she drops the dollar on top of several more.

THE TWELFTH CHILD

On Sunday evening the moon is bright in the sky by the time they finish dinner. Ophelia suggests they take their tea on the side porch.

Annie carries the mugs to the porch, and Ophelia comes behind her with a plate of small pumpkin cakes. Each tiny cake is perfectly round and topped with sweet frosting.

At first they sit quietly, looking out on the moonlit garden. In the distance is the scarecrow Annie saw yesterday. He is wearing a plaid shirt, and the yellow of the plaid seems to be lit from within. Although he stands at the far end of the garden he somehow seems closer.

"Did you make that scarecrow yourself?" Annie asks. She already knows the answer will be yes.

Ophelia nods. "That was Edward's favorite shirt." The sound of nostalgia is woven through her words. "Sometimes late at night I look out into the garden, and if I squint real hard I can almost imagine he's my Edward."

"Edward was your husband?"

Again Ophelia nods. She thinks about telling of the tragedy but decides against it. It is something she has not spoken of for all these many years, and perhaps it is best to leave it at rest. She speaks only of the good times.

"Edward and I came to this house not long after we were married," she says. "We were out for a Sunday drive when we just happened upon it and fell in love with the place. The funny thing is," she adds with a laugh, "we weren't even looking for a house. We were looking for a place to picnic."

"I take it Edward is…" The word "dead" is at the tip of Annie's tongue when she changes it to "gone".

"Yes," Ophelia answers. "Almost sixty years ago."

For the first time in the two days Annie has been there, she sees sadness in the woman's face. It is the look of loneliness swimming to the surface. Of course she is lonely, Annie reasons, living here with nothing but a scarecrow and garden for company. Spurred on by the growing fondness she feels for Ophelia, Annie asks why she has remained in the house for so long.

"Being here all alone," she says. "Wouldn't you be happier in one of those lovely places that offer assistance? You'd have friends your own age and nice hot meals—"

Ophelia interrupts. "I'm happy here. And I'm not all alone. I've got my guests, I've got neighbors who come to the apothecary and I've got Edward."

A look of confusion wrinkles Annie's brow. "I thought Edward was gone."

"Only his body," Ophelia replies. "His spirit is still here. All the memories we made in those ten short years, they're still here."

Annie stretches her hand across the table and places it atop Ophelia's gnarled fingers. The gentleness of understanding softens her voice.

"Your memories of Edward belong to you," she says. "They'll go with you wherever you go."

Ophelia gives a knowing smile and shakes her head. "It wouldn't be the same. There's something special about this house. Things grow here. Even memories. If I were to leave here all the other memories would be lost, and in time even my memories of Edward would fade away."

"What other memories?"

This is the moment Ophelia has anticipated. For two days she has said nothing and patiently bided her time, but now this girl from Pennsylvania has asked the question that will give way to the secrets. Ophelia feels certain Annie is the one. Perhaps the girl has already felt it. It's possible that, just as Ophelia herself felt it all those years ago, Annie now senses the magic of this place.

"Most people think memories are only in a person's head," Ophelia says, "but I know better." Ignoring Annie's look of confusion, she continues. "Good memories attach themselves to an inanimate object and stay there until the right person comes along. When they find a soul that welcomes them, those memories live again."

Several seconds tick by before Annie laughs. "For a moment there you had me. I thought you were serious."

"I am serious." There is a touch of indignation in Ophelia's voice.

"That's impossible," Annie replies. "Memories can only belong to the person they happened to. They're not like germs that stick to something and get passed on."

"That's what I once thought," Ophelia replies. "But a few years after Edward was gone, I started searching my mind for memories and that's when I found them."

"Found memories of Edward, right?"

"Yes, but I also found a whole lot more." Ophelia pushes back from the table and stands. "Wait here, I'll show you."

With that she turns and disappears back inside the house.

The years weigh on her like a heavy overcoat, and Ophelia slowly climbs the stairs to the loft. She knows where she'll find the Bible; it is in the top drawer of the chest that Edward brought from their first apartment.

The chest is the only piece of that furniture Ophelia still has, and it is packed full of memories—some hers and some belonging to other people. Each object is kept in a separate drawer lest they collide with one another and lose their clarity. Carefully lifting the Bible from its resting place, she tucks it under her arm and starts back down the stairs. Going down is only slightly less arduous than going up. She is careful to first lower her right foot to the tread below and then bring the faulty left leg down beside it.

Moving slow as she does, it is a good ten minutes before Ophelia returns to the porch. When she finally gets there, Annie has a fresh pot of dandelion tea sitting on the table.

"Well, well," Ophelia says, "isn't this a nice surprise."

"I hope it's not too strong," Annie replies. "I made it just as you do. Three scoops of dandelion and a pinch of chamomile."

Although that amount of dandelion is almost double what Ophelia normally uses, she nods and says, "Perfect."

Laying the Bible to the side, she stirs a spoonful of honey into the tea and sips it. Strong, but perhaps strong is good. She has never before shared these memories because they were not hers to share. Now she has no choice; she is getting on in years, and if the memories are not passed along they could be lost forever.

There is only a spot of tea left in the cup when she leans forward and begins to tell the story.

"This Bible was the first one," she says. "I found it in a second-hand store. I'd looked at ten or more books before my hand went to this one, but the minute I touched it I could feel the memory."

Annie listens intently, but the corner of her mouth twists into an expression of disbelief.

"In that dusty old shop I could smell the cool breeze coming off a mountain and I could see the slender fingers of a woman's hand. I heard a sob as the woman dipped her pen in an inkwell and crossed out the words 'girl baby'. On top of those crossed out words she wrote in 'Abigail Anne'."

Ophelia lifts the Bible and hands it to Annie. "Look for yourself." She watches closely as Annie lifts the cover and looks at the first page.

Beneath the words "Family Bible", someone has written "William Matthew Lannigan – born September 1824 – died January 1879. Married to Hester Louise Dooley".

"There's no crossed out words," Annie says.

"Keep turning the pages," Ophelia replies.

Annie does, but before she has gone through the next two pages a chilly wind rolls across the garden and she feels a shiver go down her back. When Annie turns to the fifth page she sees the words Ophelia has spoken of. Above the name Abigail Anne is the name William Matthew Lannigan – born August 1912, the same day as the girl. They were twins.

Annie is certain that acquiring another person's memories is not possible, and yet the earnestness with which Ophelia speaks has cracked open the door to belief.

"Don't you think that maybe you only think you remember these things because you've seen it written here?" she asks.

"I saw the woman's hand before I opened the book," Ophelia answers.

"And that's why you think you've picked up memories that belong to this Abigail Anne Lannigan?"

"No," Ophelia answers. "The memories I feel belong to the girl's mother, Livonia."

Annie looks at the Bible again. Above the listing of the two births is a notation that William John Lannigan has married his fourth wife, Livonia Goodwin, in April of 1910. She flips back through several pages. The listings move from century to century—there are new wives, babies born and deaths. So many deaths. When Annie counts up the children of William John Lannigan, there are twelve. Abigail Anne is the twelfth child.

There are dates of death for many of the children but no indication of what has happened to Livonia Lannigan or her twin babies. Annie turns to the next page, but there is nothing.

She turns several more pages before she looks over at Ophelia and asks, "What happened to all these people?"

"I would imagine they're dead by now."

"Even the babies?"

Ophelia nods. "The twins were born in 1912; they'd be over 100 years old now so it's not likely they're still—"

"But if you have memories of them can't you tell—"

"I don't feel the memories of anyone but the mother," Ophelia answers. "And even then I can only feel the good memories attached to the Bible."

Momentarily setting aside her doubt that such a thing can be true, Annie asks what memories Ophelia can see.

"Not see so much as feel," Ophelia answers. "I know Livonia was happy with the birth of those babies, but there's some kind of sadness blocking out anything more."

"Knowing a mama is happy over the birth of her babies is a natural thing," Annie says. "A person doesn't have to have ESP to know that."

The corners of Ophelia's lips curl ever so slightly. "You're right about that, but there's more."

"More?"

Ophelia nods. "Yes, but it's late."

"I'm not the least bit sleepy," Annie says. "Go ahead, tell me everything."

"Everything is a tall order," Ophelia replies. "Memories aren't meant to come all at once. Squash them together and they'll become meaningless. A good memory is something you have to live with for a while, let it settle in and become part of who you are. Then when it's feeling at home and welcome, you can move on to the next one."

Annie suddenly has an urge to hear more of these mysterious memories, so she pushes on. "I'm ready now."

Without arguing the point, Ophelia takes the Bible from the girl's hand and stands. "Not tonight. We have plenty of time."

This is true. Ophelia Browne has eleven months before she will turn ninety.

ANNIE'S DREAM

When Annie crawls into bed that night she cannot rid herself of thoughts about the story Ophelia has shared. One moment she is filled with the desire to know more, and the next she is poo-pooing the idea of calling up another person's memories.

It's the rambling of an elderly woman, she tries to tell herself, but that is difficult to believe. Ophelia is a woman who despite her years is witty and bright. Age has not blurred the line between fantasy and fact. Annie thinks back to earlier in the day when they worked side by side in the apothecary. The magic was not in the herbs or potions; the magic was in Ophelia herself.

After hours of tossing and turning Annie finally drifts off to sleep, and when she does the dream comes.

She is once again sitting on the side porch, but this time she is alone. She opens the Bible in front of her, but the pages are blank. There is nothing—no words, no names, no dates.

"What did you think you'd find?" a voice asks.

Startled, she looks around and sees nothing. She is still alone. "Who are you?" she cries out.

"I'm a memory," the voice answers.

"Impossible!" Annie answers. "A memory is not a living thing. A memory is…"

The voice erupts in lighthearted laughter. "You were saying?"

The laughter sounds again.

Still searching, Annie lifts the table skirt and peers beneath it. Seeing nothing, she asks, "Where are you?" Her words are sharp and spiked with apprehension.

"I'm anywhere, everywhere, nowhere," the voice says. "I'm a memory."

"Well, you're not my memory!" Annie shouts. "Leave me alone."

"People don't get to pick and choose their memories. So it looks like you're stuck with me."

"No, I'm not!" Annie says angrily. "Go find somebody else. I don't believe in ghosts, spooks or spirits."

"I'm none of those things," the voice answers. "I'm the memory Livonia left behind."

"Then go back to Livonia, if that's where you came from."

"Ah…" The memory sighs. "If only such a thing were possible."

Before Annie can question the voice again, there is a rustling in the brush and the scarecrow steps up to the edge of the porch. There are patches of straw sticking out of his shirt, but he no longer has a cotton head. He has Michael's face.

"What's going on here?" he demands. The anger and intolerance in his voice also belong to Michael.

Annie gasps. "Michael? What are you doing here?"

"I'm a memory you have to deal with," he answers.

"No!" she screams. "No! No!"

The sound of her own scream wakes Annie, and she bolts upright. There is a moment of confusion as she looks around the room then remembers where she is. Beyond the window she sees the pale pink of a new day dawning.

◦━✦━◦

By the time Ophelia gets downstairs, Annie has made a stack of pancakes and a pot of dandelion tea.

"I hope you don't mind," she says, "but I was up early and…"

"Bad dreams?" Ophelia questions.

Annie nods. "I was dreaming about the people in that Bible." She hesitates for a brief moment then asks, "How did you know?"

"I also had dreams," Ophelia replies. "I think that last pot of tea may have been a mite too strong."

"But why would that—"

"Dandelion tea sharpens a person's sixth sense," Ophelia says. "It can sometimes enable us to see things as they really are rather than as we think they should be."

"Oh dear," Annie says. "I made this pot a bit stronger than last night's, and I've already had two cups."

Ophelia laughs. "Well, then, you've had enough dandelion tea for a while."

⚬══✦══⚬

When the clock chimes nine, Annie calls her office and tells Peter Axelrod she needs the week off. "A family emergency," she says but doesn't elaborate.

He is a bit piqued but stops short of being angry. When she hangs up she feels a weight lifted from her shoulders. There is no work, there is no Michael; there is only a full week of Ophelia and the magic of her stories.

For the first time in many months, Annie is truly happy. The anxiety that has dogged her footsteps for months is gone.

ANNIE

I'm not a person who is quick to take to new people and places, but I feel right at home here. I can't even say why. I just know how I feel.

Maybe it's the peacefulness of this place, or maybe it's Ophelia and the way she tells those stories. I don't believe a memory can stick to something and be passed along like a flu germ any more than I believe pigs can fly, but when she's talking about those memories she makes them sound as real as the chair I'm sitting in.

This afternoon she brought a snow globe from upstairs and told me it was another of her treasures. Treasures, that's what she calls these things that supposedly have memories attached to them. According to her, the snow globe belonged to the woman who wrote in the Bible; only the snow globe, Ophelia says, has lots of good memories. After lunch we sat on the side porch and she told half a dozen stories about this little girl, Abigail Anne, and her mama.

I could see the snow globe was really old and when I held it in my hands it was warm, like some kind of heat was bottled up inside of it, but I didn't feel the memories the way Ophelia does. She asked if I could see how it was—that little girl and her mama talking about dreams and planning for the future. I said I could imagine how it might be, but I couldn't see anything other than the figurine of a little girl and a Christmas tree inside the snow globe.

I'm not certain, but I think Ophelia was disappointed when I said that. In the future I should just pretend to see the things she sees. What *harm would it do? I'd be making an old woman happy, and that's a good thing. She doesn't have much else to be happy about, living alone with just a scarecrow and garden for company.*

It's funny how Ophelia talks about all these people she never once met, and yet she says hardly anything about her husband.

I wonder why.

THE BICYCLE

For the remainder of the week, they follow much the same routine. A leisurely breakfast followed by two hours of gardening and then lunch on the side porch where they sit and talk for most of the afternoon. Ophelia has a storehouse of treasures but she brings them out slowly, one at a time. On Tuesday it is a small rubber ball that she claims belonged to an eleven-year-old boy with a dog.

"I suspect there were times when that dog was his only friend," Ophelia says. "He'd throw the ball and the dog would chase after it." She hands the ball to Annie and points out the bite marks.

"See," she says. "Proof positive."

Annie nods as if in agreement, but she knows the same marks could likely be found on almost any ball belonging to a child with a dog.

"The lad's name was Adam," Ophelia says. "Adam or Allen, something of that sort."

"You can tell all that from a ball?"

Ophelia laughs. "Not just a ball, I have other things."

"Things that belonged to the same boy?"

Annie sees a smile cross Ophelia's face as she gives a nod. "I have the lad's bicycle also."

"But how?" Annie asks. "How do you find these things and know they belong to the same person?"

Ophelia's shoulders rise and fall, and there are several seconds of hesitation before she answers.

"Sometimes I find them and sometimes they find me," she says.

"The ball found me. I was planning to prune my big bromeliad that day, and when I sat down with my clippers there was the ball, stuck smack in the middle of the plant."

"But how?"

Ophelia gives another shrug. "I asked myself the same thing. At first I thought the ball belonged to some local child who'd come looking for it, so I carried it around in my apron pocket for three whole days. The third day was when I started sensing the memories that were stuck to it."

"What about the bicycle?"

"I found that in the Sisters of Mercy thrift shop."

"But how'd you know it belonged to the same boy as the ball?"

"I'd had the ball for almost a month and while I couldn't see the lad's sadness I could feel it was there, so I began worrying about him. I worried that he might be cold or hungry, hoping he had a place to sleep and someone to love him."

Annie leans closer and listens intently. There is a certain intimacy in the way the old woman speaks. Her words seem soft as a whisper; they have the feel of a secret that can travel between friends and go no further.

"That day I stopped at the Sisters of Mercy in search of an iron skillet, but the moment I walked into the shop I was drawn to the back of the store where they have things like baby carriages and bicycles."

Annie says nothing but her brows are knitted together, and she focuses on the words coming from Ophelia's mouth.

"I think it happened because I was so worried about the boy," Ophelia tells her. "I suppose he needed to let me know he was okay. Anyway, the second I touched my hand to that bicycle I knew it was his and I could feel the happiness coming out of it."

Annie gives a sigh and leans back. "Wow. That's unbelievable!" As soon as the word is out of her mouth she wants to take it back.

"I don't mean unbelievable as in not to be believed," she adds, "I mean just flat out amazing."

"That it is." Ophelia nods. "That it is."

Ophelia has already moved on to a new story when Annie asks if she can see the bicycle. Although she is reluctant to admit it even to herself, she wants to touch the bicycle and see if she also feels the memories it holds.

"It's in the storage shed," Ophelia says. She stands and motions for Annie to follow.

They leave the porch and cross the yard to where the shed stands. Annie has been here before; it is the same wooden building where Ophelia stores her garden tools and the small chair she sits on to pull weeds. Although Annie has not noticed it before, in the far back of the shed there is a blue tarp covering what must be the bicycle.

Ophelia makes her way through the stacks of flowerpots, hoes and rakes, and Annie is right behind. When Ophelia lifts the tarp, Annie is surprised. She'd pictured a shiny bright bicycle, one bursting with memories, but this, like so many of Ophelia's treasures, is old. It is a thing past its prime, rusted in any number of spots and with a front wheel that is crumpled and bent.

"This isn't what I pictured," Annie says. There is a tinge of disappointment in her voice.

Ophelia laughs. "It's not the outside appearance of a thing that makes it precious, it's what's on the inside."

Oddly enough Annie understands that she is referring not only to the bicycle but to all of life. The buds of a dandelion brewed into tea, the words written inside the Bible and most likely the soul of a person. Annie returns the smile.

"Would you mind if I touch it?" she asks.

"Of course not," Ophelia answers. She steps aside and makes way for Annie to move closer to the bicycle.

Annie wants to feel what Ophelia feels. She wants to experience the memories, but when she touches the bicycle there is only the grit of rust beneath her fingers. She moves her hand across the fender and then grips the handlebars. At that moment she first senses it: the laughter of a young boy.

The shock causes her to pull back and gasp. "Oh!"

"You felt it, didn't you?" Ophelia asks.

Annie gives a nod that is barely perceptible. "I think so."

"Try again."

For a second time Annie wraps her fingers around the handlebars. This time there is nothing. She hears nothing, feels nothing. Only the pitted surface of rusty chrome is beneath her fingers, and it is a disappointment. She remains there for several minutes, moving her fingers a bit to the left, then a bit to the right, but nothing happens.

Ophelia sees the disappointment in the girl's face.

"Memories happen as they will," she says. "It doesn't mean they won't be back. It just means they need time to grow on you."

That afternoon Annie is full of questions. She wants to know everything.

Ophelia has knowledge of bits and pieces, not enough to string together into a story. The lad is a child with many secrets. He has a dog and a shotgun hidden beneath his bed.

"There is also a woman," she says. "He calls her grandma, but his parents..." Her words trail off.

"What about his parents?" Annie asks. There is subtle urgency in her words.

"They're not there," Ophelia replies. "They're gone."

"Gone as in dead?"

"I don't know," Ophelia answers sorrowfully. "Something happened, but it's a memory I can't see." Although she says nothing more, she knows that like most people this boy keeps his ugliest memories buried deep.

Annie continues to prod, but her questions go without answers. Ophelia has told all she knows.

Before the week ends, Annie goes back to the shed three times. She wraps her fingers around the handlebars the same way she did the first time, but there is nothing. She even sits on the seat and tries to imagine herself as the boy; she wants to know why his parents aren't there and where he is going. Although she cannot say why, Annie now feels a need to know this boy.

Her doubts about a memory attaching itself to an inanimate object and waiting for the right soul have begun to waver. While she cannot say it is so, neither can she say it is not.

THE LOFT

On Sunday morning Annie packs her things and gets ready to leave. She rinses the muddy soles of her Nikes but does not pack them. Instead she tucks them into a corner of the closet. They will be there when she returns.

Although she has been here for just eight days, she has developed a fondness for Ophelia and her strange little world of dandelion tea and hand-me-down memories. The rusty bicycle is foremost in Annie's mind; she hopes to hear the sound of the boy's laughter again. For five days she has told herself that catching hold of someone else's memories is an impossibility, but the sound of his laughter remains in her head—a single memory canceling out all the rationales of logic.

They sit across from one another at the breakfast table when Annie suggests she will come back next weekend or the weekend following.

"If you don't have the rooms booked," she adds.

Ophelia assures Annie the room will be available. "I seldom have visitors for both rooms."

"Then why sleep in the upstairs loft?" Annie asks. "Wouldn't it be easier on your leg to use one of the downstairs rooms?"

"I suppose it would be," Ophelia answers, but her words carry no promise of change.

Annie reasons it is the thought of losing the income from the second room that worries Ophelia.

"If you have more than one visitor, you could have the second person use the loft," she suggests.

"Oh, I could never let a stranger sleep in the loft," Ophelia replies. "That's where my memories are."

Annie takes this to mean the collection of items Ophelia calls her treasures, the objects from which she gleans the long-forgotten memories of other people.

"You could bring your things downstairs," she suggests. "I'll help you move them."

Ophelia laughs. It is a warm sound that seems to smooth the lines crisscrossing her face. "You can't move the memory of Edward. He's up there with me."

The old woman gives a sigh that rumbles through her like the wind of an oncoming storm. Annie knows more of the story is yet to be told, and so she sits and waits.

"Edward was the love of my life," Ophelia says, and then she hesitates for several seconds. It is as if she is calling images to mind as she absently picks at a loose thread on her apron.

When the thought comes she looks up and says, "I know other people claim this husband or that husband was their one true love, but after a few years they meet someone else and marry again. Not me. After the tragedy, I never gave a sideways glance at another man. I knew there was no one else like Edward, so I had to be happy living with what was left of him."

"He sounds like a very special person," Annie says.

"Oh, he was. One in a million." As Ophelia tells of the way they fit together in one another's arms, her eyes turn from steely grey to the violet hue of her younger years.

"Edward had a sensitive soul," she says. "He could see straight into my heart."

She continues, telling of how when they first came to the house they'd take a blanket and lie in the yard looking up at the stars and talk about the plans they had.

"That first summer was absolutely perfect," she says. "I had Edward, this beautiful house and enough dreams to last a lifetime."

As Ophelia speaks it appears she is looking at Annie, but she is not. She sees a different time, a time when Edward sat in that same chair. A time when she believed things would always be as they were. It is as if she is breaking free of a reverie when she says with a sigh, "Oh, how I hated to see that summer come to an end."

Although Ophelia does not tell this part, that year she grew melancholy when frost settled on the ground and they could no longer lie together counting the stars in the sky.

Seeing his wife's sadness troubled Edward's heart, and he decided to give her a gift that would replace what she was missing. For weeks on end he spent every spare moment in the attic. Ophelia heard him up there sawing sheets of plywood and hammering away, but when she asked what he was doing he'd simply answer that he was working on a surprise. At times she'd tease him with guesses at to what it might be.

"A swing for the back porch?" she'd say. "A hope chest? A picnic table?"

Each time Edward would laugh and say only that it was a surprise.

Back then the loft was simply an attic, a place with bare rafters that framed the house and held up the roof. The only way to get up there was a folding staircase that disappeared into the ceiling when it was not being used. A few sheets of plywood surrounded the staircase and formed a small square of flooring. But if you wanted to go from one side of the attic to the other, you'd have to make your way across the two-by-fours. One wrong step and you'd come crashing through the ceiling.

Ophelia smiles; she can still see the pride in Edward's face that Christmas morning.

"We'd used all our money to buy the house, so that year we agreed not to buy Christmas presents."

She chuckles and her voice takes on the sound of happiness. "I made Edward a scarf, but I was just learning to knit so it ended up wide on one end and narrow on the other. I apologized for it being such a lumpy thing, but Edward claimed it was the nicest scarf he'd ever owned. He wore it to work all that winter."

As she listens, Annie's thoughts flash back to last Christmas when she and Michael were together. For months she'd saved to buy him that gold watch. He'd smiled and said it was nice, but three days later he took it back to the store and exchanged it for a stainless steel diver's watch that was waterproof. His gift to her had been a pair of diamond earrings with stones that probably cost twice as much as the ring she was hoping for.

"Did Edward give you a gift that year?" Annie asks.

"Oh, yes, indeed." Ophelia nods. "While I was in the parlor knitting, he was working upstairs in the attic. At times all that sawing and hammering was so loud I thought the house would come down. For almost two months Edward wouldn't say a word about what he was doing. Then on Christmas morning he brought me up there to see my gift. He'd put down a brand new edge-to-edge floor, whitewashed the walls and built a platform bed smack in the middle of the room. But best of all was this great big glass window in the roof. It was right over the bed."

Ophelia looks down at her hands and smiles as if she is seeing the memory. "Edward knew how much I missed lying out there and listening to him talk about the stars and what we'd do with our life, so he made a place where we could keep right on doing it all winter long."

Annie sighs. "How wonderful." She is remembering the diamond earrings, and they are a poor comparison to the skylight Ophelia has described.

"I'd love to see the loft," she says.

The thought of sharing her greatest treasure pleases Ophelia. She rises from her chair and motions for Annie to follow.

Ophelia leads the way up the staircase. Although she is slow, it somehow seems more fitting that she crosses the threshold first. Annie follows two stair treads behind. Anxious as she is to see the room, a tiny prickle of fear tugs at her heels and warns that she is about to step into the memories of another person.

If it is true that good memories can reveal themselves to someone else, she knows this is the time and place where it will happen.

When they step into the room it is different than Annie expects. Simpler perhaps, but with a warmth she can feel. Sunlight streams through the glass skylight and lights the room. The bed is covered in a patchwork quilt, and a rag doll rests against the single pillow. Like the quilt, the doll looks aged.

Annie points to it. "Is she one of your treasures?"

The smile that lights Ophelia's face is answer enough, but still she nods. "Jubilee's mama made that doll for her."

Annie is surprised. This is the first time a memory has been given such a definite name and an explanation. "How is it you know so much about this treasure?"

"The doll belonged to a very young girl. It's easier to gather the thoughts of a child, because they haven't yet learned to hide things."

"So you have good and bad memories from this doll?"

The bright sun moves behind a cloud, and a shadow as dark as coal dust falls across Ophelia's face. She is no longer smiling.

"Yes," she says. "There are a number of Jubilee's tears inside the doll."

Annie wants to know more, but to ask seems invasive.

When thoughts such as these come they weigh heavily on Ophelia. Years ago she was stronger and could carry the sadness on her back without bending beneath it. Now it is far more difficult.

"That's enough for today," she says and starts toward the staircase.

Annie follows her, but as she is about to leave the room she turns and looks back. For one fleeting second she sees them lying on the bed: a young woman and man. The woman is nestled in the crook of his arm, and her face glows with happiness. Annie knows she has chanced upon a memory that belongs to Ophelia.

They return to the kitchen, and Ophelia pours the last of the tea into their cups. It is nearing noon and Annie has six hours of driving ahead of her, but she doesn't rush.

"Why don't we have lunch on the porch before I leave?" she suggests.

Ophelia smiles, and the sadness she has carried down the stairs seems to fade.

"We have leftover roast chicken," she says, "and endive and tomatoes."

It is after four when Annie finally climbs back into her car and starts for home. She has a long drive and much to think about.

ANNIE

*I*t's the strangest thing, but listening to Ophelia talk about Edward as she did has made me start missing Michael all over again. I know at the end things got pretty disagreeable, but in the beginning it was good...maybe even as good as what Ophelia and Edward had.

I don't think for one minute Michael would ever build me a room just so I could look at stars, but back then he did bring me flowers most every Friday. When he passed by the grocer on Third Street he'd stop and buy one of those little bouquets from the outside stand. He'd come in with the flowers behind his back and this big old smile on his face. "Guess what I've got for you," he'd say.

I always knew it was flowers, but we'd make a game of it. I'd guess: a book, a pair of socks or a box of candy. He'd wait until I made two or three wrong guesses, then pull the flowers from behind his back. When he did I'd squeal, "Lilies! My favorite!" No matter what bouquet he had, I'd say it was my favorite. Those were good times, not just because of the flowers, but because we had fun being together.

On Saturday night we'd usually go out to dinner. More often than not we went to Luigi's, a little Italian restaurant where you brought your own bottle of wine. It was just a six-dollar bottle of wine and two plates of spaghetti, but I'd sit there thinking I was the luckiest girl in the world.

Luigi never rushed us. Every so often he'd come by with some special little offering—a cappuccino, a tiny plate of chocolates or mints—and give us this all-knowing grin. "Is good when young peoples is in love," he'd say.

After Michael got the promotion we started going to fancier places, places with a dining room captain and more silverware than you could ever use. But it was never the same as Luigi's.

A few months back I got to thinking about Luigi's and went there figuring I'd stop in and say hello, but the restaurant was gone. It's now a Chinese nail salon. I asked the girl at the desk if she knew where Luigi had gone, but she just shrugged and said she "no understand English so good".

When I think of all the good times we had, I'm kind of sorry I kept at Michael about getting married. Maybe if I hadn't done that we'd still be together.

I wonder if Ophelia and Edward ever argued about things like that. Probably not, but I sure would love to know.

TWINS, FINS & MERGERS

When Annie arrives home there are eight messages on the answering machine. Four are from Peter Axelrod, her boss at Quality Life. Two are from her friend, Sophie. One is a recorded sales pitch from an investment company, and the last is from Michael.

"Where are you?" he asks, that all-too-familiar tone of impatience thick in his voice. "Call me, I've got something to ask you." The message ends with a click. There is nothing more; no explanation of what he wants to ask.

For a brief moment Annie allows herself to think it might be the question she waited years to hear, but recalling the tone of his words she knows such a thought is foolish. His voice wasn't the sound of a suitor looking to propose; it was that of a man wanting to know if his suit is back from the cleaners. Annoyed. Impatient.

Still warmed by the afterglow of her visit with Ophelia, Annie is in no mood for another confrontational discussion and clicks past the message. Instead of returning Michael's call, she calls Sophie.

Before the second ring, Sophie picks up the receiver. She has caller ID so she knows it is Annie.

"Where have you been?" she asks.

It strikes Annie odd that she often goes for a week or more without a call from anyone, and now both Sophie and Michael have asked where she's been.

"I was only gone for a week," she says. Her words have the sound of an apology.

"You should let *somebody* know when you're going away," Sophie replies. The somebody she refers to is herself. "I called your office and they said you were out for the week. It struck me strange that you'd go away without saying a word, so I asked the receptionist if she was sure it was Annie Cross she was talking about."

Annie laughs. "I'm the only Annie there."

"Yes, but to leave without telling me…"

"When I left I thought I'd be back on Monday, but as it turned out I was having such a good time I decided to stay the week."

"Did you go to Atlantic City without me?" Sophie asks accusingly.

"No, Burnsville. It's a small town just past Richmond."

When Sophie asks what is in Burnsville, Annie tells of her visit with Ophelia. After she tells of the memories found in Ophelia's treasures, she says, "Imagine a potpourri that gives off the fragrance of whatever you like."

"Maybe that's what I need," Sophie answers, "because all I'm smelling around here is dirty diapers." From there she launches into a lengthy story of what a terrible week it has been. The twins, she claims, have been almost unbearable.

The twins are toddlers, both boys, and both with the pale blonde hair of their daddy. Annie finds it hard to sympathize with Sophie's complaint, because she would trade places in a heartbeat. Sophie has what Annie wants: a loving husband and two adorable babies to hold in her arms.

For the first time in months Annie is truly happy and she is anxious to share the stories of how she looked back and saw a young Ophelia in the arms of her Edward, how she felt the tinge of life in the rusted bicycle. She wants to talk about the magic to be found in growing things, but Sophie gives her no chance.

"The boys have been on a tear," she says, "and does Craig care?" Without waiting for Annie to answer, she adds, "Not a twit! You're lucky to have a job where you can take time off and escape."

When Annie tires of listening to her friend's complaints, she says she's got to go. "It's late and I've got other calls to make," she claims.

The truth is she has no other calls to return. She has mentally crossed Michael off the list, and Peter Axelrod will not be in the office until tomorrow morning. Little by little the happiness Annie brought home fades. All four messages from Peter were about a backlog of case files, and the last one suggested she would have to work late every night this week to catch up.

Annie is an actuarial. Although she sometimes feels she has no life of her own, she spends her days figuring out the odds of other people living long enough to enjoy theirs. She evaluates each life based on factors such as smoking, use of alcohol and family history, but happiness is nowhere in the calculation.

Annie thinks it should be. Surely people with a lot to live for are more likely to stick around for a longer time. Ophelia Browne is a perfect example.

Before Annie can wash the day from her face and slip into her pajamas, there is a familiar knock on the door. He does it as he's always done it. Three short taps, a short pause and then two more. The radio is playing so he knows she is at home. She hesitates for almost a minute and the tap, tap, tap comes again.

"Just a minute," she calls out, then crosses the room and opens the door.

Without bothering to say hello, Michael tells her he's been calling all week and asks where she's been.

"On vacation," she answers without further explanation.

Perhaps the answer is somewhat unexpected, because he stops and looks into her face. "That must be it. You look really good! Where'd you go, the Caribbean?"

Annie laughs. "No, Burnsville."

What Michael notices is actually there, but Annie hasn't yet seen it. Her cheeks are pink from gardening in the sun, the muscles in her face relaxed and softened; she is wearing a glow of happiness.

"Where's Burnsville?" he asks.

"South of Richmond," Annie answers. "I was visiting a friend." She says nothing more. The truth is that she doesn't want to share the stories of Ophelia with Michael. He is a cynic and won't believe them anyway.

Michael explains he's there because he left his snorkel fins on the top shelf of the closet, but after he has retrieved them he makes no move to leave. There is a glint in his eye, and on three separate occasions he tells Annie how good she looks.

Annie smiles and thanks him for the compliments, but she does nothing to encourage him to stay. She is afraid of herself. Michael has a smile that draws her in, and the memory of his arms around her is still fresh in her mind.

Before he leaves Michael flashes that smile and says it's great to see her.

"I've missed you," he adds, and it almost sounds sincere.

"It's nice to see you too," Annie replies.

She doesn't give him a smile, but he sees the look in her eyes and it is enough. Michael is certain the door is still open.

"Maybe we could have dinner one night," he suggests. "Catch up on old times."

Annie is unprepared for this and she simply echoes, "Maybe."

Almost immediately she knows this is a mistake.

⚓

Her desk is piled high with case files when Annie arrives at work Monday morning. On top of the pile is a note from Peter. It reads, "See me when you get in." There is no signature, just a large P at the bottom of the note.

It is not yet eight o'clock, and Peter Axelrod seldom comes in before nine-thirty. Annie sets his note aside and opens the first folder. Hopefully by the time he arrives she will be able to report that some of the policy evaluations have been completed.

She has gone through the first three folders when a newcomer walks in and settles into the desk next to Annie's. She is wearing a black suit that makes Annie's grey slacks look drab by comparison.

"Good morning," Annie says.

The woman drops her purse into the desk drawer then comes over and extends a hand.

"Hi," she says with a smile. "I'm Kathryn Newman, Metropolitan Underwriting."

Annie extends her hand and returns the smile. Were it not rude to do so she would have asked what the woman was doing here. Instead she offers only a "Nice to meet you".

With that Kathryn Newman turns back to what is seemingly her desk and sits down. In front of her there is a stack of files taller even than the pile on Annie's desk. Kathryn opens the first folder and begins reading.

Annie can hold back no longer. "Are you new here?"

Kathryn gives a shallow little laugh. "I guess you could say that."

Since there is no further explanation forthcoming, Annie returns to her work.

At five minutes after nine Peter dashes through the door looking a bit winded. As he passes Annie's desk, he gives a nod that signals she should follow him into his office. She does. Once inside, he closes the door behind her.

"You picked one hell of a week to take off," he grumbles. "I tried calling your cell and couldn't get through. Where were you?"

"A small town south of Richmond. The service there is spotty at best." She doesn't mention her cell phone was turned off. "Who's this Kathryn Newman?"

Peter nervously rubs his chin, catching it between his thumb and forefinger.

"Not good news," he says. "It looks like Metropolitan may be acquiring us. Henley's saying it's a merger, but Metropolitan's the one calling all the shots." He stops, reaches into the desk drawer, pulls out a roll of Tums and pops two in his mouth.

This is not a good sign. Annie has worked with Peter for seven years, and she knows his acid indigestion flares up whenever there is trouble.

"So, what's going to happen?" she asks. "Are we all about to be fired or something?"

"I'm sure there's gonna be duplication of duties, but I don't think they'll get rid of the lot of us." His tone is more nervous than reassuring.

When Annie returns to her desk she is more aware than ever of Kathryn. It seems as if the woman has grown several inches since she walked up and introduced herself. After seeing the worried look on Peter's face, Annie now wonders if Kathryn is there to spy on her, to watch her work and report any tiny little misstep.

Setting the completed files in her approved basket, Annie moves on to the next folder. Her mind is no longer focused on how long Samuel D. Breckenridge will live; she is now wondering if she'll lose her job.

EVERYTHING CHANGES

In one single week the environment in the office has reversed itself completely. What was a laid-back, easygoing workplace is now electrified. No one lingers in the lunchroom. Peter gobbles Tums like they are peanuts and Henry Scaliger, a man who always enjoyed a martini with his lunch, now nibbles a tuna fish sandwich at his desk. The only one who looks happy is Kathryn Newman.

Sitting at the desk next to Kathryn's grates on Annie's nerves. Although the woman seldom looks up from the stack of files she is poring through, Annie feels she is being watched. It is a logistical impossibility, but she can almost swear Kathryn's left eye roves around while her right eye is focused on the files.

Annie is a number cruncher. The job pays well but is emotionally draining. People who live in Alaska or Kansas or Oklahoma, mothers and fathers she's never seen, are reduced to sets of numbers. Add the numbers and guesstimate how long they'll live. Take off a few years if they smoke, add on a few if they belong to a gym. Never mind that they have a family to provide for, a Boy Scout Troop to lead or a church choir to sing in. Annie's job is to ignore all those things and whittle each applicant down to the number of years they are expected to live. It matters not if they are sinner or saint.

This is not the type of thing she wants to do. Were it not for the sizable rent on the apartment, she would welcome the opportunity to be laid off. She'd volunteer to be the one to go so Peter might keep his job. In the middle of assigning a number to a father of six from Baltimore,

Annie's thoughts drift back to Ophelia's garden. Suddenly she has a great longing for a cup of dandelion tea.

She pulls a card from her handbag and studies it. In the center of the card is a likeness of the sign in front of Ophelia's house. She picks up the phone, dials the number and asks if she can come back again next weekend.

"I can be there late Friday," she says, "but I've got to come home Sunday night." She considers telling Ophelia about what is going on in the office but decides against it. The situation is like a bad memory, not something to be shared.

When Ophelia says she'll be glad to see Annie there is a musical sound to her voice. Annie wants to go right now, but of course she can't. There is Kathryn's roving eye, Peter's nervous stomach, the rent on the apartment and...

On Thursday afternoon shortly after two o'clock an announcement comes across the paging system. It says there will be a company-wide meeting in the boardroom at 4:30. Attendance is mandatory for all personnel.

"This is it," Ken Jefferson says with a moan. He is thinking of his wife, three kids and a mortgage that has to be paid every month. He pushes the stack of lab reports he's been reading to the side and looks up the phone number for the unemployment office.

Similar scenarios happen throughout the office. Bob Kramer actually calls a headhunter and asks if the position in Secaucus is still available. Barbara Mosier slips out, dashes down to the lobby and buys a copy of the *Inquirer*. She stuffs it into her purse then heads for the ladies room. There in a stall, where she is hidden from view, she turns to the Help Wanted section.

Few if any employees work. Within Kathryn's line of sight, Annie makes a valiant attempt to look busy but the truth is she's been staring at that same file for nearly an hour. Finally she writes a quick assessment that assigns this father of five a number that estimates he will live to be an old man. It will lower his life insurance premiums. Annie thinks not of the accuracy of the number but of the five children this man will one day leave behind.

At four-thirty when everyone gathers in the boardroom, they stand shoulder to shoulder. There is barely room to breathe, but the crackle of tension and smell of fear have both managed to squeeze themselves in.

James Henley, the CEO of Quality Life, makes the announcement. It is now official: Kathryn Newman is the new managing director of what will be the Quality Life division of Metropolitan Underwriting. Henley's statement is brief, but he makes it clear that he expects everyone's full cooperation in moving the transition forward in a smooth and efficient manner.

Peter stands alongside Henley and nods agreement, but Annie notices the twitch in his right eye.

After Henley's matter-of-fact announcement, he steps aside and Kathryn moves into the spot. She is confident and speaks in crisp clear tones. She first thanks Henley for placing his trust in her; then she turns to the group and begins to talk about the future.

"As we move forward," she says, "we will consolidate departments only where consolidation is warranted." She continues for several minutes, assuring everyone that his or her job is secure. No one believes her. Tom Neely from accounting nervously taps his fingers against the side of his leg, and his secretary is blinking back tears.

When Kathryn finally concludes her speech, there is a short burst of applause and a whispered sigh of relief. For now there are no layoffs.

Annie is not crazy about her job, but neither can she afford to be without it. She assesses her options. Give up the apartment and look for a smaller place on the south end of town. Maybe move to Cherry Hill. She's got some money saved, but with a rent twice what she can afford it will go fast. She considers the possibility of finding a roommate, someone who would share the expenses as Michael did, but that thought lingers for only a few moments. It is a one-bedroom apartment—a large one-bedroom—but a one-bedroom nonetheless. No roommate would be interested in sharing a king-size bed. That arrangement is only for couples, and Annie is no longer one half of a couple. She is single and alone. It is a discouraging thought.

When the workday ends, the office clears out quickly. It is as if the inevitable has already happened and the workers are anxious to move on. Although Annie has worked late almost every night since her return, she also leaves at the stroke of five. She plans to draw a steaming hot bath and soak in it until the water has grown cold and her fingertips are wrinkled as washboards.

On her way home Annie stops at The Feathered Duck and buys a takeout meal of General Tso's shrimp with vegetables. It comes with soup and an eggroll. It is a luxury she can afford now but perhaps not in the future.

She is in the house less than five minutes when there is a familiar rap on the door. Annie is not in the mood for Michael. She no longer wants to hear that he's forgotten his swim mask or tennis racquet or left a single sock behind. He is a reminder of what she has lost, and as she stands on the edge of losing yet more she needs no such reminders.

She ignores the knock until it comes for a third time. Obviously he is not leaving. She crosses to the door and opens it. Michael is smiling, and his hands are held behind his back.

"I've got something for you," he says. "Guess what it is."

"I have no idea," she answers wearily.

"Oh, come on," he urges, "just take a guess. Any guess."

"A bucket of beans." Her answer is meaningless, but Annie has a lot on her mind and is not in the mood for games.

"No, flowers!" He pulls his right hand from behind his back, and in it he is holding a bouquet of yellow roses.

Yellow roses are truly Annie's favorite flower, but she doesn't give the reply he expects. She takes the flowers from Michael and then looks into his face. "Thank you."

There is a moment of awkward silence before she asks if he would like to come in.

"I've got to put these in water," she says and leaves him standing in the living room as she heads to the kitchen.

She is still trimming the stems when he comes up behind her and wraps his arms around her waist. He leans across her shoulder and whispers in her ear. "I thought maybe we could have dinner together."

When she doesn't answer he adds, "I was going to suggest Luigi's, but the place is closed down. It's now a—"

"Nail salon," Annie cuts in. It touches her heart that he remembers.

"You know?" Michael asks. A note of surprise is in his voice. "I thought that was our special place. Don't tell me you went there with somebody—"

"It's not like that," Annie says. "I just happened to pass by a few weeks ago and noticed the nail salon. Too bad." She sighs wistfully. She does not tell him she went there to see Luigi, to try to recapture a few moments of the happiness they'd known.

"Is there another place you'd like to go?" Already he is assuming that her answer is yes, that she will, as she has always done, fall willingly into his arms.

"I don't know if having dinner together is such a good idea," Annie says. "We've both moved on and perhaps we should leave it that way."

The words she speaks are the far from the truth. Annie has not moved on, but she is trying. To allow Michael back into her life would mean losing what little ground she's gained.

He tightens his grip on her waist and leans so that his face is snuggled into the curve of her neck.

"I haven't moved on," he says softly. "I miss you, Annie."

When he twists her around she stands facing him. He pulls her to his chest, lowers his face to hers and kisses her. Softly. Gently. In a way that is both caring and promising.

"At least have dinner with me," he says.

"Just dinner?" Annie asks cautiously.

He nods then adds, "Unless you want it to be more."

With very little persuasion, Annie agrees to go. She takes the bag from The Feathered Duck, sets it in the refrigerator, then excuses herself saying she's got to freshen up. She disappears into the bedroom and closes the door behind her. She questions whether Michael will try to follow, but he does not.

It takes only a few minutes to change from the grey slacks to a black dress, a dress that is both simple and stunning. Annie chooses the dress because she remembers it being one of Michael's favorites. She makes a feeble attempt to convince herself that's not the reason for picking this particular dress, but when she stops at the mirror to apply lip gloss the image looking back wears a disapproving frown. For a brief moment Annie can swear she sees the crinkle of Ophelia's eyes in the reflection.

"Impossible," she mutters and returns to the living room.

ANNIE

*P*erhaps it's not the smartest thing in the world to let myself get involved with Michael again, but the sad truth is I miss him something terrible. My life feels so empty without him. Walking through the park with a man who's got his arm snuggled around your waist is a lot different than walking through the park alone.

Michael and I were good together. The problem has never been our attraction to one another; it's been that we want different things. I'd like to get married and have kids. Three, maybe four. Not Michael. He says having kids drives a wedge between a man and woman. His theory is when kids enter the picture they get all of the woman's attention, and the husband becomes nothing but a meal ticket.

"Take Mark Dowling," he said. "That man hasn't had a night out with the guys in ten years." I argued that Mark and Cindy seem very happy together, but Michael insisted it was just Cindy who was happy. "How can a man be happy when he's tied to a wife and six kids?" He made it sound like a question, but I knew Michael well enough to realize it was more of a statement and I didn't bother answering.

Last night Michael said he's a changed man, but he didn't go into specifics. I was itching to know exactly how he'd changed, but we were having such a good time I hated to spoil the evening by asking. I felt like I was with the old Michael. The one I fell in love with, not the one who went at me tooth and nail every time I so much as mentioned marriage.

Near the end of our being together most dates ended with us angry at each other. We'd go out for a quick dinner and be back home before ten *o'clock, But last night was different. We went to a little French restaurant where there was a violinist and a tiny dance floor. Even though there was not another soul waltzing around the parquet, Michael asked me to dance—three times! Knowing how he's always hated to be the only couple on the dance floor, I would say that's a sure sign he's changed.*

When we came home he asked if we could go out again Saturday night, but I had to say no. I told him I was going away and wouldn't be back until late Sunday. I suspected Michael would ask where I was going, and he sure enough did.

"Visiting a friend," I told him.

"Male or female?" he asked.

I told him it was a female but didn't mention her name. I figure he doesn't need to know about Ophelia and her ability to pull memories from things. He wouldn't believe it anyway. Michael's a skeptic; he doesn't believe in much of anything.

It's funny because Ophelia is the exact opposite. She believes in everything. I think that's what makes her so likable.

A Job in Jeopardy, A Love
Renewed

The clock has already struck one when Michael kisses Annie goodnight and disappears down the hall. Once he is gone, she pulls her suitcase from beneath the bed and starts to pack. Tomorrow she will leave from the office rather than return home.

Already the excitement of revisiting Memory House is running through her brain. She thinks of the bicycle. She remembers how it felt when she touched the handlebar; the boy was there, reaching out to her. The image came and went in less than a heartbeat, but it was solid as the bicycle itself.

Twice Annie has visited an antique shop on the south side of town. She has wandered through the dusty aisles, picked up a doll, a weathered hat and brass plated desk set, but none of these items offered up memories. They sat lifeless in her hands, revealing nothing of their past history.

She has now come to the conclusion that the secret to such insight is only at Memory House. If she is to gather memories from other times and places, Ophelia must show her the way.

As Annie closes her eyes, her last thoughts are surprisingly not of Michael but of the lovers she saw lying on the platform bed in Ophelia's loft.

⁘─◆─⁘

Annie arrives at the office early. She plans to skip lunch and be out of there by three-thirty. She is surprised to find Kathryn is not at her desk; in fact the desk has been cleaned out. Not a single file or notepad remains. It is a small measure of relief not to have Kathryn's roving eye watching her.

Pleased with this turn of events, she settles at her desk and reaches for the file atop a new pile. It is an application for a joint policy—a husband and wife with a handicapped child. They are asking for a policy that guarantees one million dollars if either of them are injured or killed.

Annie suddenly feels something. She is not sure if she is picking up a memory or if it is just her heart reaching out. The husband has high blood pressure and the wife smokes, but Annie bypasses those factors and gives them both a rating that will allow them to obtain the policy.

She is working on the fourth application file when she hears the shrill of laughter. The sound comes from Peter's office, but when Annie steps into the aisle and peers around the corner it is Kathryn sitting behind the desk that for all these years has been Peter's. He is nowhere to be seen.

The nameplate on the glass window now reads Kathryn Newman, Managing Director.

A frown settles on Annie's face. Peter is not only her boss; he is also her friend. There has been no mention of change, but already it has begun. Annie's suspicion is that he has been moved out of his office to make room for Kathryn.

Going in search of him, she walks the full length of the office floor checking to see if he has been moved to another office or, worse yet, is sitting in one of the small cubicles at the far end of the floor. She finds him in the office in back of the accounting department, the office that yesterday housed Tom Neely. Peter is packing things in one box and unpacking them from another.

"What's going on?" she asks.

Peter gives the pretense of a smile. "Henley needed an office for Kathryn and asked me to move."

"Where's Tom?"

Peter shrugs. "Gone, I guess."

"Gone as in laid off?"

"Probably." Peter lifts Tom's calendar and tucks it into the box. "Kathryn said it was his choice."

"I doubt that," Annie says angrily. She pictures Tom Neely, a soft-spoken man with silver hair and a pleasant disposition. He is no match for someone like Kathryn.

Approaching the subject gingerly, Peter tells Annie she will now be reporting to Kathryn.

"She wants tighter control of the underwriting department," he explains.

This news is not what Annie wants to hear. She rolls her eyes in disbelief, then asks what Peter is going to do.

"I'll work with accounting," he says.

"Work with or manage?" Annie asks.

Peter lifts a set of bookends from the box he has been unpacking. "That's yet to be determined." He avoids looking directly into Annie's eyes.

"This stinks," Annie says then turns to leave.

"Be careful," Peter warns. "Kathryn's not a woman you want to cross."

When Annie returns to her desk she still has seven case studies waiting for her, but she plows through them and is finished by one-thirty. All seven have been given a generous rating. With her workload squared away, she heads for what is now Kathryn's office.

From the doorway Annie sees the tight twist of hair atop Kathryn's head, but her chair is turned and her back to the door. She is studying a file and doesn't hear Annie approach. With little patience and a growing dislike for Kathryn, Annie raps against the doorframe. Without waiting for a response, she walks in and stands in front of Kathryn's desk. It is an aggressive move, but Annie doesn't care.

"I've got to leave early today," she says. "Family problems."

Kathryn turns her chair slowly, glances up and then returns her eyes to the file. She is slow to speak but eventually says, "My understanding is that you are single and live alone."

"That's true," Annie answers, "but I've got an elderly aunt in Burnsville. She's not well and needs help."

"And you feel this aunt is more important than your job?"

The question rattles Annie's bones, and she answers too quickly.

"Yes, I do," she says, making no apology for her words.

Without speaking Kathryn removes the wire frame glasses perched on her nose and looks square into Annie's face.

"This is not the time for arrogance," she says. "You may take the afternoon off, but be aware that we are all under considerable scrutiny at this time."

Kathryn has included herself in the "all", but Annie knows this is not true. Everyone else in the office may be under what she calls scrutiny, but Kathryn herself is not. She is the one wielding the axe.

Annie mutters a simple thank you and returns to her desk. Five minutes later she is in the elevator and on her way to the parking garage.

◦━✦━◦

The thought of Peter settling into the small office picks at Annie's brain until she sees the skyline of Philadelphia disappear in the rear view mirror. Only then can she let it go. There are worse things, she tells herself. Poor Tom Neely has no job at all. Annie remembers Peter's words—"It was his choice"—and she hopes Tom was offered retirement. Retirement doesn't carry the same stigma as being fired.

Once she has put that issue to rest, she moves to thoughts of Michael. She wants to believe he is a changed man, but how much he has changed is yet to be determined.

For the first time in many months she is now able to remember the sweetness of his kiss and the warmth of his arms around her. How, she wondered, could she have forgotten these things? Again Annie tries to liken her relationship with Michael to that of Ophelia and Edward, but there seem to be few similarities.

Give it time, she tells herself and brushes back the doubt hovering over her hopes.

The corner of Annie's mouth curls upward as she pictures Michael's look of disappointment when she said no to a Saturday night date. It was the first and only time she could recall him having that look. Right from the start it had been the other way; she was always the one offering up her heart, and he was the one deciding whether to accept it.

Annie is happy with the changes in Michael. She believes it will breathe new life into their relationship. What she doesn't yet realize is that she also has changed.

A HOLE OR A WHOLE

Annie arrives in Burnsville two hours earlier than she'd anticipated. Lost in her thoughts, she's driven straight through and not stopped for anything to eat. There has been no lunch or supper, and the rumble of her stomach now reminds her of it. She slows the car as she passes the weathered sign, then pulls into the driveway and climbs out. Rapping the brass doorknocker, she wonders what memories Ophelia will reveal this time.

It is a full minute before the door swings open, and Ophelia offers a welcoming smile. She is wearing a large bib apron that has a dusting of flour on it.

"Sorry," she says, "I wasn't expecting you until later."

"I left the office early," Annie explains. "A lot of problems there."

Annie leaves it at that. She has decided to ask for advice on the troubling situations, but not just now. This moment is reserved for the simple joy of returning.

As they pass through the foyer, Annie catches the scent of beef bubbling in thick brown gravy. "Are you making stew?"

Ophelia laughs. "You must be hungry."

"Yes, I am," Annie answers. "And I can smell—"

Ophelia turns and points to the glass bowl on the table. "It's the potpourri."

Annie laughs and smacks her forehead. "I forgot."

"Well, I hate to disappoint you," Ophelia replies, "but I've made a roasted chicken. I thought maybe we'd have a late-night supper on the porch."

Walking back toward the kitchen Annie sniffs the air again. This time she catches the fragrance of warm chicken and can picture it, the skin a crispy brown and the meat so tender and juicy it falls from the bone.

"I guess the potpourri knows what I'm thinking," she says. "Now I'm smelling chicken and sweet potatoes."

Ophelia chuckles. "That's not the potpourri; it's my roasted chicken. When you knocked, I was just taking it from the oven."

"Sweet potatoes too?"

Ophelia nods.

In the kitchen Annie moves about as if this is her home. There is familiarity in everything she touches. Filling the water kettle, she sets it to boil then reaches for the canister of dandelion tea.

"I have been dying for a cup of this," she says.

Her words are strangely enough true. Several times during the week Annie longed for the bittersweet taste in her mouth, so much so that on Tuesday she stopped at the gourmet grocer on Liberty Street and bought five different boxes of tea, all herbal. Not one of them came close to the taste of dandelion tea. In fact the alfalfa tea was so bitter that after a single sip she tossed the entire box into the garbage can.

As Annie moves about, folding napkins and setting silverware in place, the stress on her face is obvious. Her brow is furrowed, and ridges of worry stretch across her forehead. She smiles, but her mouth is a tight little line that exposes the truth.

Ophelia notices this and pulls a bottle of lemon balm from the cupboard shelf. In even the most extreme cases lemon balm will calm the nerves, but it is a potion to handle carefully. Add too much and the person will fall into a deep sleep that lasts for days. Counting the drops as they fall, she adds nine to the tea then pours a cup and hands it to Annie.

As they settle at the table, Annie gives a deep sigh. With it she lets go of the week's frustration.

"It's wonderful to be back here," she says.

Ophelia smiles. She doesn't say anything but she doesn't have to; her smile is enough. It encourages Annie to give voice to the thoughts in her head. Although she planned to wait until tomorrow, the words tumble from her mouth.

"It's been a strange week," Annie says. "Good in some ways, bad in others."

"I believe it best to speak of the good first," Ophelia says. "Once a person has good thoughts in mind, the bad often seems less stressful."

Seeing the wisdom in such a strategy, Annie tells of Michael's return.

"I've been miserable for months," she says. "Then there's a knock on my door, and he's asking to come in. He says he's missed me. A lot."

"What about you?" Ophelia asks. "Have you missed him?"

"Have I ever!" Annie answers. The enthusiasm in her voice adds emphasis to the words. "Being alone isn't fun. The days drag and—"

"Oh, I understand being alone," Ophelia cuts in. "After Edward was gone, this house seemed emptier than I thought possible. It was as if the rooms had grown larger and I had become smaller."

Annie leans forward and drops her chin into the valley of her hands. "I know exactly what you mean. That's how I feel. It's only a one-bedroom apartment, but sometimes it feels way too big for me."

"The thing is," Ophelia adds, "there's a big difference in missing someone because they filled a hole in your life and missing someone because they were your whole life."

Such a thought stops Annie cold. "How can you tell the difference?"

A softness settles on Ophelia's face, and she smiles as if at that very moment she is seeing Edward.

"Your heart tells you," she says. "When a man is your whole life you will do anything for him, no matter how foolish or how difficult. You'll even give up the things you love and follow him to the far ends of the earth without ever asking why such a thing was necessary."

For a long moment Annie says nothing. She is thinking about Michael, remembering that he wanted to be with her this weekend and recalling how she'd said no because she wanted to be here. Not with Michael, but with Ophelia.

"What about the other people in your life?" she asks. "Aren't they important?"

Ophelia can still see the tears cresting her mother's eyes and the puffed-up redness of her daddy's face.

"Yes, they are," she says, "and leaving them behind can be painful beyond belief."

"Why do you have to leave them behind?" Annie asks. "Shouldn't a woman be able to have both?"

"You would hope so," Ophelia says with a sigh, "but it's not always possible."

For a moment she is silent, gathering her own memories. When the picture is set in her mind, she tells Annie of how her father disapproved of her marriage.

"Daddy thought Edward was a penniless dreamer," she says. "A man who would never be able to support a family."

"But he did," Annie interjects. "You have this house and—"

Ophelia gives a gentle laugh. "It's always easier to see things when you're looking back." She continues her story, telling how they'd run off and been married by a justice of the peace.

"That was something Daddy couldn't forgive," she says. "He never spoke to me again. When that happened, we left Atlanta and settled in Richmond."

"That's so sad." Annie's shoulders slump as she leans back into her chair.

"No question it caused a great deal of sadness in my life," Ophelia says. "But it still wasn't enough for me to leave Edward."

After she has said this Ophelia sits silently. Her eyes, now misty, focus on the hands in her lap. She rubs the fingers of her right hand across those of her left and touches the ring finger that once wore a band of gold. She must once again pack away these memories. They have been with her for over half a century, and yet they still ooze pain when brought to the surface.

Annie, oddly enough, is relieved that she has no such worries. After her mother's death, her daddy remarried that same year. He and his new wife live in Florida and have no interest in what Annie does one way or the other.

When they have finished eating, Annie carries two mugs of hot dandelion tea to the side porch and they sit in the wicker chairs. It is nearing the end of May but on this night there is a chill in the air, so she wraps her fingers around the steaming mug and warms them. She asks if Ophelia would like a woolen lap robe, and the answer is yes.

Unlike her office, the things at Memory House have not changed. Everything is exactly as it was on her last visit, so Annie knows she will find the throw neatly folded and draped across the arm of the sofa. She fetches it and tucks it around Ophelia's bony knees.

The moon is a slender sliver in the sky but the stars are bright. Annie closes her eyes, and for a moment she can see the youthful Ophelia and Edward lying on the platform bed in the attic. They are looking up at this same sky.

Perhaps it is the magic of the stars or giddiness of too many cups of tea, but she finds courage enough to bring up the subject she has pondered all week. She begins by telling of her visits to the local antique shop and the disappointment of holding objects and finding no memories.

"I was wondering if you might be able to teach me how to find the memories," she says.

Ophelia laughs. "Not everything has a memory attached to it. A feathered hat might be simply that, no more, no less. Perhaps it was one that sat on a closet shelf, never worn for a special occasion, never given a memory."

"But what if these things did have a memory attached and I simply failed to feel it? Maybe if you taught me how to—"

"It isn't something that can be taught," Ophelia cuts in. "It's almost unexplainable. People with an open mind and great sensitivity just seem to be born with it."

Annie hesitates for a moment then recalls the number of difficult cases that have crossed her desk; situations where a life insurance policy was needed and the person's qualifications were less than stellar. Many times she could sense the urgency of those people. Although they were nothing more than names on an application, she could feel their pain.

"I think I have a fair level of sensitivity," she stammers.

"I think so too," Ophelia says. A smile curls the corners of her mouth.

"Well, then," Annie asks, "how do I get the ability to find memories?"

Ophelia lets go of the smile she was holding back and chuckles aloud. "I think you already have the ability." She explains that she suspected it when Annie first put her hands on the handlebars of the bicycle.

"I felt the shock," Ophelia says. "It was a jolt of electricity, the kind a person gets if they shuffle their feet across a carpet then touch a metal light switch."

Annie's eyes are wide with amazement. "Did you hear him laugh?"

When Ophelia nods, that is all it takes.

Annie wants to know everything there is to know about the bicycle boy. "What is he like? How old is he? Where does he live?"

Although she wants to look inside the boy's memories, Ophelia has nothing more to give.

"I've told you, his name is Allen, or Adam, something like that. I've only a few memories about him, and I've told you all I know." Ophelia smiles. "I think the boy's memories are meant for you. The answers are there, but it's up to you to find them."

A determined look settles on Annie's face as she sips the dandelion tea that has now grown cold.

"That's what I'm going to do," she says. "That's exactly what I am going to do."

A plan is already forming in Annie's mind.

ANNIE

I know it seems strange that I would pass up a Saturday night date with Michael to come here, but there is a certain magic in this place. It draws me back. Maybe it's listening to Ophelia talk about Edward, or maybe it's because I halfway believe that I too might be able to gather some of the memories left behind.

When I put my hands on that bicycle, I heard the boy's laugh. There's no question about it. You can rationalize all you want and say it might have been the wind or the laughter of a nearby neighbor, but I know for sure it was the boy. I can't say how I know; I just do.

Granted, Ophelia has a special gift for things like this, but if the bicycle was willing to give up its memory to a nobody like me then it means something. I'm starting to think the boy has a message for me. Some kind of secret he figures I ought to know. It might sound like I'm crazy as a loon for chasing after this, but the truth is it's exciting. It's the same as searching for buried treasure; there's one chance in a million you'll find it, but the possibility of that chance is stuck in your mind so you keep searching.

Anyway, even if I don't find out anything, I like being here with Ophelia. When I'm with her I can just be me. I don't have to try to be smart or witty like I do with Michael. I can relax and say whatever pops into my head.

Ophelia never makes me feel like I've said something wrong. When I told her about how much I was missing Michael, instead of saying that's flat out dumb pining after a man who walked out on you she explained *how a man can fill the hole in your life or be the whole of your life. That makes a lot of sense. I used to think Michael was the whole of my life, but now I'm beginning to wonder.*

I can tell he's changed, but I've got to question how much. I've seen him wine and dine a customer he can't stand and the whole while he's acting like the guy is his best friend. The truth is Michael does what he has to do to get what he wants.

Loving such a man is stupid, but it's hard to remember that when he's kissing me. Coming here this weekend is a good thing. It puts some breathing room between me and Michael...hopefully enough that I won't let my heart run away with my head again.

Rust is the Reason

On Saturday morning Annie gets out of bed before the sun has cleared the horizon. By the time Ophelia comes into the kitchen Annie has already downed three cups of dandelion tea and a cinnamon croissant. She sits at the table with a notepad and a list of the items she'll need.

"Where's the nearest hardware store?" she asks.

Looking a bit puzzled, Ophelia answers, "About two miles south of State Road Forty."

At the top of her list Annie writes SR40, 2 miles.

"What's all this about?" Ophelia asks.

"The bicycle," Annie answers. "I figured it out. The reason I can't find out more about the boy is because the bicycle is rusted and broken. It needs to be fixed."

Ophelia raises a doubtful eyebrow. "Fixed?"

Annie nods. "If I clean up the bicycle and get it in working shape I can ride it. Then I might be able to feel what the boy felt when he was riding it."

"Oh, I don't really think—"

"That's it," Annie says with certainty. "Last night I was thinking about it and remembered a cell phone I once had. It stopped working for no reason. Then I found out it was because of the rust."

Ophelia says nothing, but her expression is a one of confusion.

This doesn't discourage Annie. "After I cleaned the rust off the charger connection, the phone worked just fine."

"I still don't see what a phone has to do with—"

"It's simple," Annie says. "The cell phone wasn't working because it wasn't charging. And the reason it wasn't charging was that rust on the plug prevented it from making contact."

"How much of that tea have you had?" Ophelia asks.

"It's not the tea," Annie replies. "Just think about this. There was only a little speck of rust on that plug, but it was enough to stop the phone from making a connection. What if all the rust on that bicycle is why I can't connect to the boy?"

"Well, I suppose it could be possible," Ophelia says. "Lord knows I've seen stranger things."

"I know that's it," Annie says emphatically. "I'm positive."

There is no doubt in Annie's mind that she has figured out the answer and she is now determined to see it through. Shortly after breakfast she and Ophelia climb into the car and start toward State Road Forty.

When Annie drives for almost twenty minutes a worried look crosses Ophelia's face and she says, "We should have come to it by now."

What was supposed to be a highway is actually a flat stretch of partially paved road. On either side there is little but fields of green and cows grazing in the pasture.

"Maybe it's further down the road," Annie suggests. "It looks like there might be a cross street up ahead."

When they reach what appears to be a cross street, it turns out to be a railroad crossing.

"Oh, dear," Ophelia says. "I'm beginning to think we've gone too far."

Before they turn around and head back in the direction they came from, Annie drives another three miles. Once she has made the U-turn, Ophelia suggests they go a bit slower.

"I'm certain it's on this road," she says. "We must've missed it."

Inching along like a giant turtle, Annie drives while Ophelia keeps an eye out. They travel nine miles before she spies a strip mall up ahead.

"On the right," she says. "It looks like a shopping plaza."

Pushing her glasses higher on her nose, Ophelia begins to read the stores listed on the sign. "Highway Lunch, Hair Care, Grab and Go,

Irwin Tinsley, Dentist." Although only these four stores are listed she says, "I think this is it."

Swinging into the tiny strip mall, Annie parks alongside a car coated with a layer of dust. "I don't see a hardware store."

"I'm fairly sure this is where it is," Ophelia says. Although she claims to have shopped the store at least a half-dozen times, the sound of her voice has little conviction.

"I'll go check," Annie suggests. When she climbs out of the car she has every intention of getting directions then being on her way, but the moment she opens the luncheonette door the aroma of fresh-brewed coffee hits her. It is a smell that has the feel of familiarity. She returns to the car for Ophelia, and minutes later they are sitting on two of the six stools at the counter. They are the only customers.

"Hello?" she calls out.

"Be right with you," a voice answers.

It is several minutes before a bearded man hurries out from the back. "Sorry, I had business to attend to."

Annie orders two coffees, then turns to Ophelia and asks if she would like a sweet bun. "Maybe one of those frosted doughnuts?"

Ophelia gives a broad smile and nods.

When he sets the coffee in front of them, the counterman asks, "You ladies from around here?"

"I am," Ophelia answers, "but Annie here is a Pennsylvania girl."

The man looks at Ophelia, and for a moment it seems as if he is studying her face. "I figured I knew every soul in Burnsville, but I don't think I've seen you here before. Herman Fetters." He stretches his hand across the counter.

Ophelia lifts her hand and shakes his. "Ophelia Browne." Before he can turn away, she asks, "Didn't there used to be a hardware store here?"

"Ten, maybe twelve years back," Herman replies. "Ed Langer had a hardware shop where Doc Tinsley's got his office."

"Ten years?" Ophelia gives her head a sorrowful shake.

"Maybe twelve," Herman says. "It's been a while."

Annie orders a second cup of coffee. As much as she loves Ophelia's dandelion tea, she misses the rush that comes with a mug of coffee. As Herman refills both cups she asks, "Do you know where we can find a hardware store?"

Herman fingers the snow-colored hair on his chin then says, "I think the closest one's over in Langley."

"How far is that?" Annie asks.

"Twenty miles, give or take." Herman turns back to Ophelia. "You ought to stop by more often. We got a lunch special that's real good."

"Maybe I will," Ophelia replies and returns the smile.

Now armed with a new set of directions that will take them back to where they started and then over to Route 97 East, they return to the car. As Annie backs out of the parking lot and pulls onto the road she gives Ophelia a knowing grin.

"That Mister Fetters was flirting with you," she teases. "And it seems to me you were flirting right back."

"That's preposterous," Ophelia says, but the flush of her cheeks is obvious.

They have no trouble locating the Ace Hardware store on the main street of Langley. When Annie asks about the best rust remover for use on chrome, the clerk hands her a bottle of Rust-Be-Gone.

"This'll do the trick," he says. "Pour a bit on a square of aluminum foil and rub gently."

"Aluminum foil, like Reynolds Wrap?" Annie questions.

He nods. "I've got steel wool if you want, but it'd scratch the tar out of whatever you're working on."

"A bicycle," Annie says.

"Bicycle, huh? Lotta work if it ain't nothing but a bicycle." He explains that the Rust-Be-Gone costs nine dollars, and he's got some nice clean used bikes that are only $10.50.

Annie explains that what she's working on is not just a bicycle, it's a very special bicycle. She says the tires are flat so she'll also need an air pump.

"Pump's eight-fifty," the clerk replies. "You sure you wanna do all that work and spend an extra seven bucks to fix up an old bike when I got a really good Huffy that's ready to go?"

"I'm sure," Annie says. She is tempted to explain how she is trying to reach back through time and find the boy who originally owned the bicycle, the boy who's laugh she has already heard, but she doesn't. She recalls her own disbelief when Ophelia first suggested such a thing and she knows the clerk will be equally skeptical.

When they arrive home it is nearing noon, and Annie is anxious to start working on the bicycle. She plans to skip lunch, but Ophelia won't hear of it.

"By the time you get the bicycle out and change into your work clothes, I'll have lunch ready," she says.

Ophelia is happy to do this. It has been too many years that she has sat alone and nibbled on a tiny plate of goat cheese and sliced pear. It is good to have someone sitting across the table. It is good to have someone to talk with and do for. It is good to look into violet eyes that are still the color hers once were.

Ophelia knows that given the amount of rust on the bicycle the girl will be working all afternoon and be lucky to finish before nightfall, so she brews a larger pot of dandelion tea. While the tea steeps she adds a dose of pennyroyal to sweep away the weariness that will come from Annie's task.

The years have taught Ophelia that no matter how hard you try it is not always possible to get more of a memory than the object is willing to share. As she waits for the tea to brew, she thinks back on the year she first read the Lannigan family Bible. She had the same determination Annie now has. For hours on end she would sit silently, holding the Bible in her hands, waiting for it to tell her the rest of the story. Nothing more ever came of it. The Bible whispered a handful of secrets in her ear and then went silent. Whatever else there was to tell would forever remain with Livonia Lannigan.

The day has turned warm, so Ophelia pours the tea into a pitcher filled with ice and carries it to the porch. From there she can see Annie has already pulled the bicycle from the shed.

"Lunch is ready," she calls out.

Annie waves and says she'll be right in.

Ophelia nods and waves back.

At lunch Annie tells Ophelia that she's looked at the bicycle and the rust is not so deep it can't be cleaned. She lowers herself into the chair then says, "It's mostly the handlebar, and maybe a few spots on the wheels that need work." Before she takes her first sip of the chilled tea, she begins explaining how she will fold pieces of aluminum foil into thin strips to clean the areas around the rusted spokes.

Ophelia is happy listening to Annie, and as the words cross the table she gathers the warmth of the conversation. It is the first time she has ever had another person willing to look for the forgotten memories.

"I wish you could come back more often," she says.

"I do too," Annie replies. "Maybe if I had more time I could get to know everything there is to know about..."

She hesitates. It no longer seems right to call him bicycle boy; she needs to give him a name. "Allen," she says.

"I'm not certain that's the boy's name," Ophelia warns.

Annie laughs. "I know, but I have a feeling it is."

Ophelia shakes her head and chuckles. "Few people have the gift of finding memories. You're one in a million."

"Maybe a billion," Annie replies. "I don't know a single soul other than you who can do it."

Ophelia laughs again. "I guess you could say we're two of a kind." The words are barely out of her mouth when the thought brings another one to mind, a way to perhaps bring the girl back more often. "That's sort of like being related. Wouldn't you agree?"

"I suppose so." Annie smiles, the pleasure from such a thought obvious.

"Good," Ophelia says. "Seeing as how we're practically related I can't possibly accept money for you staying here, so you can come as often as you like without paying for the room."

Annie looks up wide-eyed. She is in a business where money is the measure of everything. She is a person who hangs a price ticket on people's lives. The thought of not paying strikes her as odd.

"Why would I not pay?" she says. "Renting out bed and breakfast rooms is your business."

Ophelia laughs. "It's actually more like a hobby. Folks coming and going keeps me from feeling lonely. I don't really need the money. Edward left me more than enough to live out my years."

"But you said you had to scrimp and save to—"

"We did. But Edward was a life insurance salesman, and he believed it was unfair to ask others to buy something he didn't buy himself. When he died the house was paid off, and there was money to spare."

Annie notices this is the first time Ophelia has given voice to the mention of death. Up until now Edward has always been just "gone". Feeling the friendship that is being offered, she pushes her chair back, stands and comes around to the other side of the table. With both arms around Ophelia's narrow shoulders she leans forward and kisses her cheek.

"Thank you," she whispers, and it is all that needs to be said.

All afternoon Annie works on the bicycle. Starting at the very same spot where she heard the boy's laughter, she works on cleaning the handlebar. It is slow going. She pours a dollop of Rust-Be-Gone on a square of foil, then scours the area with quick circular motions. When the spot is free of rust, she wipes it with a soapy rag, then rinses and dries it. As each area is cleaned she holds her hand to it and listens for a sound, any sound. Laughter, yes, but maybe something more. A word. A phrase. A name. But even when there is not a speck of rust or single pit mark left on the handlebar, she hears nothing.

Late in the afternoon she moves to the chrome of the pedals. Twice she hears an automobile pull into the far end of the drive, and minutes later the jangle of the cowbell sounds at the door of the apothecary.

Annie knows Ophelia is there and will offer some special magic for whatever the person needs. She wishes there was a potion to find the boy's voice, but for that there is none. There is only the magic of one soul reaching out to another.

When she finally completes the fenders Annie's fingers are cramped and the skin on her hands covered with grime. Worse yet, it has grown too dark to continue working. There is only a small bit of dusky pink left in the sky, and she still has the wheels to do.

Reluctantly she returns the bicycle to the shed. As she carefully tucks the blue tarp into place, she says, "Goodnight, Allen. I'll be back in the morning." It is as if she is talking to the boy himself.

THE GYPSY'S PREDICTION

W hen Annie left Philadelphia she planned to seek Ophelia's advice on the situation at work, but a full day has passed and she has yet to mention it. When they sit down to supper she has cleaned the grime from her hands but has not rid her mind of thoughts about the boy.

Ophelia has made a German dish of noodles and pork. This, she claims, was Edward's favorite. Annie understands why; the dish is thick with cream and settles in her stomach comfortably.

As they eat Ophelia speaks of Edward, not as if he is dead but simply gone—gone in the way of someone who is fetching a newspaper and will be back any moment. When she tells of how he could at times eat two or possibly three helpings of this favorite dish, her voice is soft and round.

Looking wistfully at the large serving bowl on the table she says, "Knowing how much Edward liked my pork noodles, I'd make three times this much and it would be gone in a day or two."

She looks back at the memory no one else can see and laughs even though it would appear there is nothing to laugh at. "He used to take a big bowl of it over to Widow Cassidy and thought I didn't know. How could I not know when Ida Cassidy washed the bowl and returned it to me every time?"

She chuckles again. "I'm pretty certain Edward knew it wasn't really a secret, but we both had a lot of fun pretending it was."

Annie could sit forever and listen to the stories of Ophelia's life with Edward. There is warmth in them, magic almost, and one story inevitably leads to another. As she listens Annie thinks back on her own life with Michael, and there are few if any such stories. They had good times and bad times but no single time that jumps out and says "This is a moment you'll remember for the rest of your life".

As Annie is thinking, Ophelia moves to another story. This one is about the staircase leading to the loft.

"It took Edward three months to finish it," she says. "Before we had the staircase I had to pull down those rickety attic steps to get up there." She hesitates a moment then with a sad smile adds, "When I told Edward I didn't feel safe going up and down those wobbly steps, he started building that staircase the very same week."

"He certainly took good care of you, didn't he?"

"Yes, he did." Ophelia gives a deep sigh; it is heavy with the weight of her memories. "After he was gone, I used to wish I'd died right alongside of him. Take me too, Lord, that's what I used to pray. Without my Edward life just didn't seem to be worth living."

Annie is like a sponge, soaking up every word. She leans in, transfixed on the calm grey of Ophelia's eyes. In them there is no look of pain; there is only a peaceful acceptance. A contentment Annie has seldom seen in her own eyes.

"How'd you get past it?" she asks.

"One day at a time," Ophelia answers. "At first I'd stay in bed for as long as I could stand it; then when my bones ached from lying there, I'd get up and go fix myself a bowl of cereal or a can of soup."

Annie can almost see the memories Ophelia speaks of, but she's uncertain if it is her power growing stronger or the old woman's way of weaving magical threads through the memories.

Ophelia continues her story with the tale of a gypsy dressed in red, gold and silver, a woman who for fifty cents looked at the palm of her hand and told what her future would be.

"It had been a wonderful day at the fair, and I was flushed with excitement," Ophelia says, "so naturally I expected her to tell me we were going to live happily ever after and have a flock of adorable babies. But that's not what happened."

The expression on Ophelia's face grows solemn as she describes how the gypsy predicted she would live a long life but death would come and bring a terrible loneliness.

"I was eager enough to believe the good things," Ophelia explains.

"But when it came to hearing about such loneliness, I told the woman she must've made a mistake. No mistake, she said, and pointed to a tiny crease across my palm. That, she swore, was a sure-fire indicator."

Ophelia tries to force a laugh, but it is a sad shallow sound. "I told Edward such a prediction was poppycock and I didn't believe a word of it. I tried to convince myself as well, but it was too late. The fear of what she'd said was like a worm eating at the inside of me. For months I tried to erase that line from my hand. I used a pumice stone and rubbed it across the palm of my hand until it was almost raw, then I took to massaging it with cocoa butter. Nothing worked."

Ophelia extends her hand and points to the line. "See? It's still there."

Annie looks at her own palm and compares the two. "Everybody has that line. See, here's mine."

Ophelia lowers her head and studies the palm Annie holds up. "Yours is different." She points to a spot between the thumb and forefinger. "See, my line points down; yours points up."

Annie looks again and sees that what Ophelia has said is true. "So you knew Edward was going to die?"

"Not at all," Ophelia answers. "I thought it was Mama the gypsy was talking about. After Daddy died Mama and me got to be real close. We didn't live close but we'd send letters most every day. I was all she had left. For months on end she'd write and tell me how poorly she was feeling. Every time I got one of those letters I'd think back on what the gypsy said and worry myself to death thinking about Mama. Finally I told Edward I've simply got to go visit her."

There is a long pause before Ophelia tells of how she bought a train ticket and went off to visit her mama in Atlanta. "I left on a Wednesday and Edward promised he'd be waiting at the train station when I got back on Sunday."

She stops speaking, pulls a hankie from her pocket and dabs at her eyes. Several minutes pass before she continues. Wiping back the tears, Ophelia tells how she arrived at the train station and Edward was nowhere to be seen.

"I was in a panic," she says. "I waited an hour and then took a taxi cab home. I didn't care that it cost seventeen dollars, the only thing I could think about was Edward. I told the taxi driver to hurry, but the ride home seemed to take forever. The whole while I kept praying Edward had just mixed up the days and forgotten to meet me."

That day comes back and Ophelia can envision it. Her chin begins to quiver, and she raises a hand to her face as if to stop the flow of tears. It is useless.

"After all these years," she says through a sob, "I thought I could speak of that day and it wouldn't be so painful."

Annie pushes back her chair and comes around to Ophelia. She kneels beside her and wraps her in an embrace. "You don't have to do this. I understand."

For several minutes Ophelia allows the tears to fall; then slowly they come to a stop. There is great sorrow in her voice when she finally speaks.

"I've not told anyone the full story of what happened, but now it's time."

She continues, telling of how she arrived home to find Edward dead. As she speaks there are pauses between the thoughts; it is as if images of that day pass through her mind and she gathers the courage to go on.

"Although Edward never told me of it, he apparently had a weak heart," she explains. "The coroner said he'd most likely been dead for two days."

Thinking she has heard the worst of it, Annie gives a sympathetic sigh. "I'm so sorry."

"I'm sorry too." Ophelia's voice is thick with the sound of regret. "Sorry I wasn't here to save him. When I found Edward he was in the loft, lying on that bed he'd made and facing toward the window. His eyes were wide open. For years I kept wondering if he was looking at the stars and wishing I was there to save him."

Before Annie can say anything, Ophelia pushes her chair back and stands. She scoops up the two dishes and carries them to the sink. Annie follows along with the teapot and butter dish. They stand with their backs to one another, Annie at the refrigerator, Ophelia at the sink, when Ophelia adds one last thought.

"Doctor Kelly said it was a massive heart attack that supposedly happened in a few seconds. He claims it wouldn't have made any difference whether I was there or not."

There is a *thunk* as Ophelia lowers the frying pan into the soapy water; then she adds, "No matter what Doctor Kelly says, I know it would've made a difference if I was there beside Edward."

OPHELIA

*S*peaking of Edward's death brings back memories I thought were dead and buried. Those were terrible times; times so bad there's not even a way of describing them. Although the smell of death was all over that loft, I called Doctor Kelly and told him to come quick because Edward had stopped breathing.

I suppose I was hoping that by some miracle they could breathe life back into him, but of course such a thing wasn't possible. After I called the doctor, I went back to the loft and sat beside Edward. I kept thinking maybe there was something I could do for him. Maybe he'd wake up and ask for a glass of water or an aspirin. Now I can see how foolish such thoughts were, but back then I didn't have the ability to think rational. When the person you love more than life itself is gone, your heart and mind are filled with sorrow and bitterness.

I blamed myself for not being here, and I blamed Edward for building that damned loft. No matter what anybody said, I knew if he wasn't up there he would have called for help and he'd still be alive. For almost two years, I didn't even step foot on the staircase. I left everything exactly as it was. The sheets crumpled and laying half on the floor, the imprint of Edward's head still on the pillow and the lamp beside the bed still turned on. Eventually the bulb burned out and the loft was like a black hole that had swallowed up my reason for living.

Two years to the day it happened I was moping around the house and thinking of all I'd lost when I heard voices coming from upstairs. At first I thought it was a burglar or some vagrants who'd snuck in looking *for a warm place to sleep. Not caring if I lived or died anyway, I grabbed the poker iron and started up the stairs. I pushed open the door, and there wasn't a soul in the room. I looked in the far corners and behind the eaves, but nothing. Then clear as a bell I heard Edward's voice.*

"Opie," he said, "it's time to start living again."

Opie is what he used to call me. Nobody but Edward ever used that name, so I knew for sure it was him. Anyway, I would've recognized his voice no matter where it came from.

At first it was scary, hearing a voice from out of nowhere, but then I started listening. With Edward's help I began remembering all the good things that happened right there in that room. All the dreams we had and the plans we'd made. It was sad that we didn't have time enough to do all those things, but I still had memories of the fun we'd had just planning. That's more than some people ever get.

That same day I put a new bulb in the lamp, changed the sheets and plumped the pillows. It felt like I was getting rid of the death in the room and making a place for good memories to settle in. And in time that's what happened.

For months I'd spend all afternoon sitting up there, waiting to hear Edward's voice again. I never did hear it as clear as I did that day, but I could always sense he was there, still looking after me.

The following spring I moved all my things up to the loft and started renting out the downstairs bedrooms.

It was about a year or so later when I learned I could hold things in my hand and bring back memories of Edward; then I discovered he wasn't the only one who'd left sweet memories behind.

The day I found the Bible that belonged to Livonia Lannigan, I knew there'd be more. Unlike people, memories don't die. They latch onto something and wait for a new person to come along and claim them.

A CROOKED WHEEL

On Sunday morning Annie doesn't take time to brew tea. As soon as daylight filters into the sky, she is back at work on the bicycle. With squares of aluminum folded into narrow strips she works her way around the front wheel, spoke by spoke. In certain spots the rust refuses to let go, and it takes three or sometimes four scrubbings before the shine comes through. The rust, when it finally does dissolve, doesn't disappear. It turns to a thick black sludge that lodges beneath Annie's nails and stains her skin. Twice she has brushed her hair back from her face and now has traces of black sludge streaked across her forehead.

When Ophelia wakes and finds Annie is already at work, she brews a pot of dandelion tea then fills a mug and carries it outside.

"I thought you could use this," Ophelia says and offers Annie the mug.

"Could I ever," Annie replies. She unfolds herself from the squat she is in, grabs a rag and wipes the grime from her hands. Allowing herself a short break, she stops working and sips the tea. With a proud smile she says, "I'm making progress, but it's slow."

They chat for a few minutes; then Ophelia turns back to the house. She is going in to prepare a brunch and will call for Annie when it is ready.

Today it is a simple meal, one that is served cold and carried to the side porch. Blueberry scones, chicken salad and sliced peaches. There is also tea, the porcelain pot covered with a quilted cozy to keep it warm.

The chill of an early spring morning is in the air, but when Annie comes in she is damp with perspiration. She rinses her face and scrubs the grime from her hands, then joins Ophelia on the porch. From where she sits Annie can see the bicycle. The handlebar gleams in the sunlight. The grips, once black, are now grey, and in one spot there is a hole worn clean though to the metal. New grips would cost only a few dollars, but replacement is unthinkable.

Biting into a scone Annie garbles, "The front wheel's finished and it looks like new. Almost." She pauses for a few sips of tea then says, "The only thing left to do is the back wheel. That and inflating the tires."

In the hours she has spent scrubbing rust from the bicycle, Annie has come to call the boy by name. As she works she speaks to him—sometimes aloud, sometimes in a whisper that only her mind hears.

"Allen," she says, "you're gonna want this bike back when you see how great it looks." It is as if she has known the lad since the day he was born.

Her plan is to do that—know the boy. Know everything about him, including how and when he came upon the bicycle. It was a special occasion, of that she is confident. A birthday maybe. Or a Christmas when he woke and found it shiny and new with a tag that read *To Allen from Santa.*

Annie is certain when she rides the bicycle as Allen would have ridden it she will unlock the memories stored inside. It is a strange obsession, one she cannot explain, but to her the boy is as real as anyone she has ever known. She has tried to imagine his face, but it escapes her. The image Annie sees is always from the back: Allen is on the bicycle leaning forward and pedaling hard. A brown dog runs alongside.

Only once has she heard his laughter, but when she is close to the bicycle she can sense him nearby. It feels as if she could turn and see him standing there. Whether this feeling comes from her preoccupation with thoughts of him or if in fact she is connecting with his memories is impossible to say. Annie knows that if such a power is to be had, hers is not yet fully developed.

It is late afternoon when she finally polishes off the last bit of rust on the back wheel. It takes another ten minutes to inflate the tires. Once that is done she steps back and admires her handiwork. The bicycle looks good, almost as good as it would have on the day Allen received it. The blue paint is cloudy in spots, dulled by time. It is something few people would notice, but Annie makes a mental note to bring a can of compounding wax with her next time.

As she stands there a cloud that has been hovering overhead moves on, and the bicycle is suddenly bathed in sunlight. Annie knows it is now time, and she feels a swell of excitement that needs to be shared. She walks to the edge of the screened porch and calls for Ophelia.

"I'm finished!" she hollers. "Come see how it looks."

Ophelia is in the kitchen and hears the call. She is wiping her hands on a dishtowel when she steps onto the porch. "Oh my. It looks wonderful!"

Annie smiles. She is obviously pleased. "I'm going to take a quick shower, then take it for a ride. You wanna come?"

Ophelia chuckles. "We can't both ride on one bicycle."

"Sure we can," Annie answers. "I'll pedal and you can sit on the crossbar."

Ophelia is a tiny bird-like woman, smaller even than a twelve-year-old child, but the thought of such a thing makes her laugh out loud.

"It'll work," Annie says, trying to sound convincing. "Back in high school I used to ride on the crossbar of my boyfriend's bike."

Ophelia laughs like she hasn't laughed for years. "In case you haven't noticed, I'm not a high school girl."

The sound of Ophelia's laughter is contagious. It tickles Annie's funny bone, and she starts laughing. Before long they are laughing at nothing but the sound of their own laughter. It reminds Ophelia of earlier days, days when such laughter came easily. When she finally catches her breath she says, "You ride the bike and I'll come out to the road and watch."

Annie nods agreement and dashes inside.

In less than a half hour she is scrubbed clean and wearing a fresh pair of jeans. This is the same outfit she will wear to travel home. It is already five o'clock; she has time for a half-hour bicycle ride and a quick supper, then it will be time to leave.

Annie is not ready to think of the drive home. For now she just wants to spend the few remaining hours with Ophelia. She pokes her head into the kitchen and says it's time.

Together they walk down the graveled drive toward the street. Annie slows her footsteps to match the pace of Ophelia's. When they reach the end of the drive, Ophelia watches as Annie swings her leg over the crossbar and gets ready to climb onto the seat.

"Wish me luck!" Annie yells as she pushes down on the pedal and starts to move.

She eases herself onto the seat with her body leaning forward. Although she has a tight grip on the handlebar, the front wheel shimmies and veers to the left. Trying to straighten the bike, she presses her weight to the right. A moment later she is on the ground with her legs tangled in the bike.

Three times Annie tries to ride the bike, and three times she ends up on the ground. The bicycle is like a wild pony that refuses to be ridden.

After the third attempt, she discovers a bend in the front wheel. When the wheel circles around to that spot it thumps against the fender and pulls to the left. For the bike to hold steady, the wheel has to be repaired or replaced. Annie is dead set against replacing any part of the bicycle. In her mind everything has to be exactly as it was when the boy rode it.

With the palm of her hand scratched and a hole in the knee of her jeans, she admits defeat.

"Well, I guess I'm not going to find any of his memories today," she says. "I'll come back next weekend and work on that wheel."

In her voice there is a mix of melancholy and happiness. The regret of not reaching the boy seems to be offset by the thought of returning to spend yet another weekend with Ophelia.

From Ophelia there is only a smile. She has already stored a lifetime of memories, but her days in this house have grown long and heavy. She delights in the company of the girl.

ROSES, MORE ROSES

Annie leaves later than she had planned. Again the time slipped away once she and Ophelia began talking. If there is little traffic and she makes good time she might be back in Philadelphia by two-thirty, but that is the best she can hope for. If Peter was still her boss she could have waited, left early in the morning and been in the office before noon.

In the dark of night with almost no traffic, the drive is monotonous and seemingly longer than it was coming to Burnsville. The radio is no distraction, because instead of singing along as she usually does she is thinking about Ophelia and the boy.

There is much she has yet to discover about the boy, but Ophelia is old and frail. She is not someone who should be alone. On her next visit Annie will ask if there is family, someone close by, someone to check on her to make sure she is not running short of groceries or in need of a ride to the doctor. As much as Annie loves coming to visit, Kathryn will make it impossible to leave early or come in late. Annie thinks of poor Tom Neely, now without a job. She knows she should be grateful she still has her job, but oddly enough she isn't.

When she was younger it seemed a challenge, betting on how long a person would live. But now it weighs heavy on her, perhaps because she has come to care about Ophelia. Putting such a measurement on someone you love is an impossible task. Although the applicants whose paperwork crosses her desk are supposedly only names for evaluation, she has come to realize that each of them are the loved one of someone else.

Annie is crossing over the Delaware Memorial Bridge when she decides to start looking for another job and perhaps a smaller, more affordable apartment.

It is almost three in the morning when she pulls into the parking garage beneath her building. When she gets to her apartment door there is a bouquet of yellow roses propped against the door. Tucked inside the cellophane wrapper is Michael's business card.

I thought you'd be home this evening, he has written. *I waited until 1AM. Call me. We need to talk. Love, M.*

Annie carries the flowers inside and puts them in a vase. She is too tired to talk, and it is much too late to call. She lays the card on the table and tells herself she'll call in the morning. She crawls into bed, not thinking to set the alarm.

Normally Annie is an early riser. She wakes sometime between six-thirty and seven and seldom uses the alarm clock, but this day is different. It is almost four by the time she falls into an exhausted sleep, so not even the light of day sliding through the slats of the blinds wakes her.

At ten o'clock the phone rings and startles her from sleep.

Annie reaches out and lifts the receiver. Before she has time to say hello, Michael speaks. His voice has the sound of annoyance.

"What's going on?" he asks.

It takes a few seconds before Annie is conscious enough to glance at the clock. "Oh no, it's ten o'clock!"

"Yeah, it is," Michael says. "I called the office. Why aren't you at work?"

"I overslept!" Annie says more to herself as opposed to answering Michael's question. "I can't talk now, I'll call you later."

Although a shower would feel good, there is no time. She splashes water on her face, dabs on a bit of lipstick, pulls on a pair of gabardine slacks and is out the door in less than fifteen minutes. She normally walks the twelve blocks to the office, but today she hails a cab. On Adams Street a car with a flat tire creates a bottleneck, and it is ten-thirty-two when she finally makes it to the office.

Kathryn is in her office, but again her back is to the door. Annie hurries past, quickly stashes her purse in the drawer of her desk and grabs a file from the new stack sitting on the corner of her desk.

It is an application from Melissa Canter, a sixty-one-year-old woman with sole custody of her grandson. On the application he is named as her beneficiary. The reports indicate Melissa Canter has lupus, but it is controlled with medication. If Annie looks only at the numbers, this is an applicant who should be rejected. Lupus is at best unpredictable.

Twice she reads the report. She sees more than the words on paper. She sees a grandmother who worries that she will not live long enough to raise the twelve-year-old boy. Annie stamps the file "Approved" and moves it to the other side of her desk.

She is working on the second file when the phone rings. Certain it is Michael, she lifts the receiver and says, "I don't have time to talk right now."

"Make time," Kathryn says. Her words are sharp and her tone no-nonsense.

"Oh," Annie exclaims, "I thought you were somebody—" Before she can finish the sentence, Kathryn is gone.

Gathering her courage, Annie heads for Kathryn's office. This time she doesn't rap on the doorframe but stands waiting patiently until Kathryn motions her in.

"Is there an excuse for this morning's tardiness?" Kathryn asks.

This time there is no arrogance in Annie's answer. "It wasn't intentional. My alarm clock didn't go off."

Kathryn gives a sigh of impatience. "That's not much of an excuse. I'm trying to help you survive this merger, but you're not making it easy."

"I'm sorry," Annie says. "It won't happen again."

"See that it doesn't."

Believing the conversation over Annie turns toward the door.

"I'm not finished," Kathryn says sharply.

Annie turns back and waits.

"I've reviewed some of your cases, and you've got a good feel for applicant evaluation," she says. "This isn't an easy business for a woman, but prove to me that you're on my team and you could go far." The phone rings and before Kathryn answers it she adds, "With Peter gone, I'm going to need a chief underwriter."

As she lifts the receiver she dismisses Annie with a wave.

When Annie returns to her desk, she is filled with conflicting emotions. At one time she would have done most anything for such an opportunity, but things have changed. There's no joy in the thought of being on Kathryn's team, and she's uncertain as to whether she even wants to be in this business. Or, for that matter, in Philadelphia.

Most of her day is spent catching up on the workload, and it is close to five when she finally gets time enough to return Michael's call. The first thing she says is "I'm sorry". She tells him of her conversation with Kathryn.

"Wow," he says, "That's great!" He suggests they go to dinner to celebrate.

Annie doubts there is reason for celebration but the thought of dinner with Michael is appealing, so she agrees.

He arrives at the apartment fifteen minutes early, and again he has something hidden behind his back. "I brought you something. Guess what it is."

He is recreating the old game they played, and this time Annie goes along with it.

"A box of candy," she says.

He shakes his head. "Guess again."

"A puppy."

"Wrong again," he says and produces a second bouquet of yellow roses from behind his back. As he hands them to Annie, he pulls her into his arms and whispers that he misses being with her. Although she is wearing a dress he's seen a thousand times before, he tells her she looks lovely and when they leave the apartment building he wraps his arm around her waist and snuggles her close.

"I've missed you," he repeats, and his words carry the sound of sincerity.

He has the evening planned. First there is dinner in a quaint French restaurant, smaller by half than Luigi's but three times pricier. He orders a bottle of pinot noir and tells the waiter they will share a chateaubriand. Only after the waiter has left with the order does he ask if that is okay with Annie.

He is remembering the things that were special in the earlier days, so she of course approves. Back then the red wine was an inexpensive Chianti and the steak was a porterhouse, but the intimacy of this moment is as it once was. He stretches his arm across the table and takes her hand in his.

As they wait for dinner he talks of the good times. The summer they rented a beach house; the weekend visits to the aquarium; dinners at Luigi's; late night walks in the park. He says nothing about the problem that drove a wedge between them.

Even as he eats, his eyes are still on her face. "Remember that weekend in Manhattan? Dinner in the Rainbow Room."

Annie's mouth is full but she nods and gives him a smile that says, yes, I remember.

"I don't think I've ever danced as much as we did that evening." He sips his wine then adds, "We should do it again."

It is a sweet thought that Annie does not know how to answer.

"Things have changed," she says wistfully.

There is a heavy pause before Michael answers. "They don't have to. It can be the same as it was before." He again takes her hand in his and his voice is softer. "Over these past months I've come to realize how much I need you, Annie. My life is empty without you. I miss the fun we had together, I miss making love to you, I miss—"

Annie interrupts. "My life was pretty empty when you left."

Her words have a sharp edge to them. Even though she has moved on, the pain of those months is easily remembered.

"I know." The smile has left his face, replaced by a mask of penitence. "I was a jerk, and I'm sorrier than you can possibly imagine. It was the biggest mistake I've ever made. Take me back, and I swear I'll spend the rest of my life making it up to you."

Annie does not expect this and stumbles over her words. "I don't know if I'm ready for this."

"Just think about it," he pleads. "Give me a chance. That's all I'm asking for is a chance. You'll see I'm a changed man."

The only thing Annie can offer is the promise to think about it, which is what she does.

ANNIE

*H*ave you ever been in a place where everything was absolutely perfect, and yet inside your head you hear a voice screaming at you to be careful?

That's how I feel right now.

Michael says he's a changed man, and to tell you the truth he acts like he is. Everything about tonight was special. Letter perfect, you might say. But that's how Michael does things. There's no halfway mark.

I'd be happy if he brought me one rose, but instead he brings a dozen. Not just a dozen, but a dozen from the most expensive shop in town. The thing is when a man gives you a single rose he's telling you he loves you, but with Michael I'm not too sure what the message is.

Before this past week, I hadn't heard from him for four, maybe five months. Now all of sudden he wants to start seeing me again.

I want to be happy about it, I honestly do, but it's hard to forget those last few months we were together. He couldn't find one nice thing to say, and when we went out to dinner he'd gobble down his food so he could get home in time to see some sports show on television.

Those months were horrible enough, but then when he walked out all he left was the note on the table saying he wouldn't be back. We never had a discussion about it, never said goodbye, nothing. After almost seven years, I thought I deserved a lot more than a note. All those months I sat alone in this apartment, thinking he'd call, but he never did. I cried myself to sleep every night for over a month.

You know what the stupid part is? Even though I can remember all these things, there's a piece of me that still wants him back. Michael can charm the skin off a snake when he wants to, that's why I've got to be careful.

Even though I'm tempted to let myself love him again, I'm not ready right now. I'm not ready to love him, and I'm not ready to walk away either. I'm hoping we can continue to see each other but take it slow. Before I let Michael back into my life, I've got to know he's sincere.

I've finally moved on to the point where I've found a bit of happiness, and I certainly don't want to go back to where I was.

Can you blame me?

THE DECISION

As the week progresses, it appears that Michael is indeed a changed man. He begins to call her twice a day, and on Wednesday they go to dinner again. Michael suggests Hung Foo's, which comes as a surprise to Annie.

"I thought you didn't like Chinese," she says.

"I know you like it," he answers.

Annie recalls only one other time they'd gone to a Chinese restaurant; that was back when they first began dating. It was a place she'd suggested and he'd agreed to, but when dinner was served he'd picked at the food and left most of it on the plate. Remembering this she suggests a steakhouse that is just six blocks from the apartment.

Michael grins and says that's a much better idea.

On Thursday when he calls the apartment at six-thirty and Annie is not yet home, he calls her at the office.

"I was worried about you," he says.

It seems strange that a man who left her to fend for herself five months ago is now worried because she is an hour late coming home from work. Annie thinks this but says it is nice of him to care. When she tells him she's catching up on work, he asks how much longer she'll be.

"Another hour or so," she answers.

"Okay, I'll pick up groceries and have dinner waiting for you," he says. Michael then asks If the spare key is still on the ledge above the apartment door.

Annie hesitates for a moment. To allow him this liberty is like reaching into a beehive for honey and knowing you're likely to get stung.

"You don't have to bother," she says. "I'm not sure what time I'll get home and there's no sense—"

"It's no bother," he says. "I don't want my girl going hungry."

The more Annie offers up excuses, the more insistent Michael becomes. When she tells him the spare key is no longer there, he says "No trouble" and suggests he can have Joe, the doorman, let him in.

"That's okay isn't it, babe?" he asks.

"I suppose so," she answers.

She says this because there is a part of her that wants their relationship to be as it once was, but somehow this seems too much too soon. Annie is afraid of rushing into something she can't handle. Scars of the last time around are still too fresh. She remembers the countless times she gave in to something simply because Michael wanted it that way.

She stays at the office a half-hour longer than she intended, and by the time Annie packs up and starts for home she's decided to tell Michael he's got to slow things down. Love isn't a faucet to be turned on and off at will is what she'll say. This speech is set in Annie's mind, but when she steps inside the apartment Michael comes and wraps his arms around her.

He has dinner waiting and has set two small candles in the center of the kitchen table. As they eat he talks of plans for one thing and another. Maybe they'll rent a beach house for the summer, or they can take a cruise together. Although Annie is caught up in the energy of his thoughts she notices that they are *his* thoughts. *His* plans. He has not once asked what she wants of this relationship.

"I don't know that I'd want a beach house," she says. "It means we'd be there every weekend, and there are other things I might want to do."

He laughs. "What's better than spending weekends at the beach?"

"I have a friend I like to visit," she says.

Michael's eyes narrow and he cocks his mouth to one side. "What kind of friend?"

"An older woman," Annie says. "She owns the bed and breakfast where I stay, and we've become good friends."

Michael raises an eyebrow and gives a look of disbelief. "You're kidding, right?"

"No, I'm not kidding," Annie says indignantly. "I'm entitled to have friends of my own. Other interests."

The look of disbelief is still stretched across Michael's face. "This is where you've been going every weekend?"

Perhaps a bit of Ophelia's resilience has rubbed off on Annie, because she feels the fire of anger sizzle and pop inside of her.

"I don't owe you an explanation," she snaps.

"Yeah, you do!" Michael says. "I'm trying to make this work while you're taking off every weekend and giving me a cockamamie story about visiting some old lady."

"I'm not giving you any story!" Annie shouts back. "I don't have to. We're not married!"

"Oh, so that's what this is all about? We're back to the marriage and kids crap, huh?"

"Get out!" Annie screams. "Get out, and don't come back!"

"Don't worry, I won't!" Michael storms out and slams the door so hard the frame shakes.

Once he is gone Annie sits at the table and cries. She cries until the candles are burnt to a nub and the food has long ago grown cold. When the tears stop Annie throws the food into the garbage can and cleans up the kitchen.

Although she climbs into bed, sleep is impossible to come by. In the smallest hours of the morning Annie goes from being angry to thinking about the things that bring her happiness. Michael is not on the list. The apartment is not on the list. And oddly enough neither is her job.

By the time daylight creeps across the horizon Annie has made her decision.

It is twenty minutes after nine when Annie arrives at the office. She is dressed in jeans and a tee shirt that boasts *Virginia is for Lovers*. She doesn't bother going to her desk; there is nothing she needs to retrieve. No pictures, no cute souvenirs, not even a pot of ivy. Although she has worked here seven years she has accumulated nothing but an endless stack of files waiting to be processed. Perhaps she has not surrounded herself with personal memorabilia because she has always known this job was a temporary stop in her life.

There is no anger in her face when she taps on the doorframe of Kathryn's office.

"Excuse me," she says, and Kathryn looks up.

Kathryn's eyes narrow in a hard glare. "That attire is inappropriate for the office."

"I'm not staying," Annie replies. Without an invitation she walks into the office and sits in the chair in front of Kathryn's desk. "I'm here to resign. After a considerable amount of thought, I've decided this job is not right for me."

Kathryn's face is pulled tight with a look of astonishment. "Did you not understand I'm considering you for the position of head underwriter?"

"I understood," Annie answers. Her voice is calm, pleasant almost. Now that this woman is no longer her boss, the playing field has been leveled.

"The job comes with a substantial pay increase," Kathryn adds.

"I figured it would," Annie says. "But if I'm not happy with what I'm doing, no amount of money will change that."

"Oh, I get it," Kathryn says cynically. "You've got a better offer elsewhere, right?"

"There's no other offer," Annie replies. "It's just that I've come to realize this isn't the type of work I want to do."

"You've been here seven years! It took you seven years to decide you didn't like what you're doing?"

Annie laughs. "I guess so."

Kathryn stands and paces back and forth behind her desk. "You've put me in a very difficult position. I was counting on you to take over as head underwriter. Now what am I going to do?"

"I'm in no position to give advice," Annie says, "but if I were you I'd get Peter Axelrod back. He's perfect for the job. He knows the business, and he's got spot on judgment when it comes to case evaluation."

Kathryn stops pacing and turns to Annie. Before she can say anything Annie adds, "Of course Peter might not be interested; my understanding is that Liberty has made him an offer."

Kathryn gives an exasperated sigh and starts pacing again.

When Annie leaves Kathryn's office she says goodbye to the handful of co-workers she is friendly with and then walks to the other end of the floor for one last visit with Peter. They chat for several minutes, and before she leaves she tells him of her conversation with Kathryn.

"I'm betting she's going to offer you the job," Annie says. "She's got her back to the wall, so hold out for more money."

As Annie stands to leave Peter's phone rings. It is Kathryn.

When she leaves the building Annie feels lighter than she has in many years. She has no job and no thoughts as to what type of job she will ultimately look for, but she is certain that whatever lies ahead will be better than what she is leaving behind. She has money enough for three, maybe four months, and for now that's enough.

She returns to the apartment and packs a suitcase. Jeans, tee-shirts, a few sweatshirts for cool evenings, some shorts for warm afternoons, sandals, sneakers and a sundress she bought last year and hasn't yet worn. This time it is not a small overnight bag but a suitcase that carries enough clothes for a week, maybe two and possibly even three.

Before she leaves she calls Sophie. They talk for almost an hour, and Annie tells her of all that has happened with Michael and her job.

"I'm taking a few weeks' vacation," she says, "but I'll be back before the end of the month. I have to do something about this apartment."

"Like what?" Sophie asks.

"If they won't let me out of the lease, I'll try to sub-let it."

"Wow," Sophie says. "I envy that kind of freedom. With the twins I could never—"

"Be glad you've got a loving husband and two great kids," Annie replies. She would gladly trade the freedom of belonging nowhere for such a gift.

It is not yet noon when Annie walks out of the apartment, locks the door and steps into the elevator. Even if the traffic is heavy, she will be in Burnsville in time for supper.

Michael has also spent a sleepless night. After he stormed out of the apartment, he regretted doing so. He now wishes he'd held his anger in check. It stood to reason that Annie would have other friends. He should have accepted it instead of going off on a tangent.

It would have been easy enough to say he'd go with her to visit this supposed friend and that would have put an end to the issue. Even if worse came to worst and he did have to go once or twice, it was no big deal. Sooner or later she'd realize that weekends at the beach were far more fun and admit he'd been right all along.

Annie is already packing her suitcase when Michael calls The Love Garden and orders a bouquet of two dozen yellow roses to be delivered to her office. He is smiling when he hangs up the receiver, confident that his plan will work. He pictures the delight on her face and starts thinking through what he will say. Not an outright apology but a softening of the battle lines. *We can work it out*, he'll suggest, and then offer to take her to dinner so they can talk things over.

Knowing Annie her voice will be cool to start with, but once he says he can't live without her and they were meant to be together she'll melt like butter in his hands.

Juan Gomez has worked at The Love Garden for almost a year. Despite the long hours and low pay he is glad for the job. It is enough to put food on the table and buy new shoes for his daughter who more than anything else wants to look like every other girl in her school.

When Juan arrives at Metropolitan Underwriting, he looks around and, seeing no other woman, walks into Kathryn's office.

"Excuse, please," he says, "where to find Miss Annie Cross?"

Kathryn looks up angrily. "Is this some kind of a sick joke?"

"No joke," he says. "Flowers for Miss Annie Cross."

"She's gone," Kathryn says. "Now get those damned flowers out of here!"

Instead of leaving he shows the delivery ticket to Kathryn. "See, is right. Where to find Miss Annie Cross?"

"How the hell would I know?" Kathryn yells. "She doesn't work here anymore! And if you're not out of my office in five seconds I'm calling security."

"Ticket say Annie Cross, Metropol—"

"Securiteeee!" Kathryn screams.

This is the first time Juan has failed to make a delivery, and he is frightened that it will cost him his job. For a good half hour he paces back and forth in front of the elevators. He is certain he has made a mistake somewhere along the line. Perhaps he got the instructions wrong. Maybe the flowers were supposed to be delivered to her apartment, not the office. He has twice before delivered yellow roses to Annie's apartment. Each time she smiled and gave him a two-dollar tip. A two-dollar tip is better than getting fired.

Since there is no other alternative he decides he will deliver the flowers to Annie Cross's apartment.

He hurries from the building and runs the whole twelve blocks to Remington Arms. When he arrives Joe waves him through. He taps on Annie's door several times, and when there is no answer he leaves the flowers alongside her apartment door and returns to the shop.

HELP AT HAND

It is six-thirty when Annie arrives in Burnsville. She wants to surprise Ophelia, so instead of calling she steps up to the front door and raps the brass knocker. Knowing Ophelia can be slow at times she waits patiently, but after several minutes have passed she lifts the knocker again. This time she bangs it hard six, maybe seven times. Again she waits.

After a few minutes with still no answer, Annie starts to worry. She looks to the far side of a budding magnolia and checks the apothecary. No light in the shop. Something is wrong, Annie is all but certain of it. She circles around the house to where the screened porch opens into the dining room that leads to the kitchen. There is a light on in the kitchen.

"Ophelia," she calls out.

When there is no answer, she calls out again and again; then she catches the scent of it—something is burning.

Annie's heart starts pounding like a kettledrum. Luckily she has pulled into the drive. She runs back to the car, pops open the trunk and grabs the tire iron. In just a few steps she is back at the front door. Swinging the tire iron, she shatters the glass panel alongside the front door then reaches through and unlocks the door. Seconds later she finds Ophelia on the floor of the kitchen.

On the back burner of the stove there is an enamel kettle, the one Ophelia uses to boil water for tea. The burner flame is on but the kettle is empty and blackened.

In a motion so fluid it seems automated, Annie switches off the burner and kneels beside her friend. Ophelia is breathing but ashen in color. Annie rolls a towel and puts it under Ophelia's head then grabs the phone and dials 9-1-1.

In a voice filled with urgency she tells the operator to send help. "Please hurry," she begs. While Annie is still on the line the operator says an ambulance is already on the way.

When Annie hangs up the receiver she returns to the kitchen, wets a dishtowel with cold water and wipes Ophelia's face and hands. When she lifts Ophelia's hand into hers the weight of it is heavier than she would have thought. Kneeling beside the woman who has become dear to her heart, Annie prays.

Her tears have already begun to flow when Ophelia's eyelids flutter open.

Dazed and confused, Ophelia asks, "Is Edward gone?"

"Yes," Annie answers. "He died a long time ago, do you remember?"

"Well, of course I remember," Ophelia replies. "But he was here. He held my hand and told me I had to keep breathing."

Annie thinks perhaps Ophelia felt her touch and mistook it for Edward's. "Are you certain it was Edward?"

"I'm positive," Ophelia replies. There is no doubt in her voice.

"Well, thank God he was here." Annie says nothing more; for Ophelia, having Edward by her side is a far greater comfort than any she could provide.

It is almost twenty minutes before they hear the wail of the ambulance siren. By then Annie has helped Ophelia up and she is sitting in the chair.

The two medics arrive with a portable oxygen tank and a medical bag. The young girl steps aside while a soft-spoken man with hair that is greying at the temples talks to Ophelia.

"Do you remember what happened?" he asks.

"Not really," Ophelia answers. "I was getting ready to make a pot of tea and I took the canister down…"

He now has a stethoscope in his hand and is listening to her heart. "Were you standing on a stool and maybe fell over?"

"I don't need a stool," Ophelia says indignantly. "The tea is on the bottom shelf."

He smiles and moves the stethoscope to her back. "Take a deep breath," he says and then asks what medication she is on.

"None." Ophelia answers.

He straightens himself and there is a look of surprise on his face. "None? I would think at your age..."

The girl hands him a blood pressure cuff, and he wraps it around Ophelia's skinny little arm.

After almost twenty minutes, he says he can find nothing wrong but suggests Ophelia see her doctor for a check-up.

"If you want we can take you into the hospital tonight, let them run some more extensive tests," he says.

Annie thinks this is a good idea, but Ophelia refuses.

"I'm fine now," she says. "I probably just had too much dandelion tea."

"Dandelion tea?" The medic laughs.

Once they are gone Annie tells Ophelia that living alone is not a good idea.

"God forbid something happens when there's no one to call for help," she says. She asks if Ophelia has family nearby.

"Family?" Ophelia laughs. "I should think not. I've outlived them all. Next March I'll be ninety years old."

"Well, then, it's time you had help. Taking care of this house, the garden, the apothecary and guests is way too much for a woman your age."

"Oh, fiddlesticks. I'm as capable as the next person. I had a bit of a dizzy spell; it's not worth fretting over."

"It was more than a dizzy spell," Annie argues. "You were unconscious for a good ten minutes, maybe more!"

Ophelia reaches across and pats Annie's cheek. "You worry too much. Worry doesn't change a thing. When it's my time to go, I'll go. This wasn't my time. I've still got work to do."

"Work? I don't think the apothecary—"

Again Ophelia laughs. "I'm not talking about the apothecary." She takes Annie's hand in hers. "You see, you didn't just stumble upon Memory House; you were meant to be here."

A puzzled look settles on Annie's face. "Meant to be here. Why?"

"I didn't know myself until this past week. I had a dream; in it there was a sun so bright I had to close my eyes. I heard a voice and it said, *You've done well, Ophelia Browne, but your work isn't quite done.*"

"Was it Edward?" Annie asks.

"Not Edward," Ophelia says. "The voice was way bigger than Edward's. I could see myself standing in front of that huge bright sun so small I looked like a speck of cinder. *What more do I need to do?* I asked."

Annie scoots closer and leans in.

It is as if Ophelia is reliving the dream. "The voice said your destiny was in my hands."

"My destiny? How?"

Ophelia gives a slight shrug. "I wish I knew. The only thing I'm pretty certain of is that one of my treasures is connected to your future."

Annie has countless questions, but she just asks, "Which one?"

Shaking her head sorrowfully, Ophelia replies, "I don't know. That's why I have to make sure you know about them all. What if I was to tell you the secret of every treasure but skipped one? That single memory could be the very one meant to change your life."

Six months ago Annie would have laughed at such a thought. But now she can almost see her life changing; changing so fast she can barely keep up with it.

"The bicycle," she blurts out. "It must be the bicycle."

"It might be." Ophelia smiles. "But I can't say for sure. There are a number of others I've not yet shared." For a moment Ophelia is still. She has so much to tell Annie, but it's not like a bag of sugar you spill on the table all at once. It has to be served up one spoonful at a time.

"It has to be the bicycle," Annie repeats confidently. "The minute I touched it I heard the boy laugh. That didn't happen with any of the others."

Ophelia sighs. "Time will tell." She lets her thoughts linger on the word "time". "If only we had more time together—"

"I can stay longer," Annie cuts in. "I've quit my job and—"

"Quit your job?"

Annie gives a grin and nods.

"What about your friend, Michael?"

Annie wrinkles her nose and shakes her head. "We're through. After listening to you talk about Edward, I've come to realize my love for Michael was never like that." She hesitated a moment then adds, "Michael wanted me, but he didn't honestly love me. We were just two people headed in the same direction, and walking together was better than walking alone. Love should be more than that."

"True indeed." Ophelia nods. "Love is more than that, and when the right man comes along you don't have to think twice."

She says this with certainty because she has lived through such an experience. She thinks back on her love for Edward. It was one that swells the heart and sprinkles stardust on everything it touches. It was one that outlasts life itself. She wants the same for Annie.

On this evening Annie cooks supper, and Ophelia sits in the chair listening to all that has happened in the past week. She chuckles when Annie tells of Kathryn and shakes her head when she hears of Michael's parting words.

When they have finished eating they move to the side porch with a pot of dandelion tea. As Ophelia settles into her chair, a devilish grin slides onto her face.

"I've been thinking you're probably right," she says.

"Probably right?" Annie repeats. "About what?"

"About me needing someone to help out." The grin stretches into a broad smile, and Ophelia asks if Annie would be willing to take the job.

"I'm your friend," Annie replies. "Remember what you said about not taking money from a friend? Especially a friend who's practically a relative."

Ophelia gives a hearty chuckle. "You've got me on that, but bear in mind I said that before I knew I'd need someone to help out."

After a bit of bantering, it is decided that Annie will stay. She will pay nothing for rent, nor will she accept money for helping.

"Once I've closed up the apartment, I'll look for a job around here," she says.

Annie's smile matches the one Ophelia is wearing.

OPHELIA

*T*he voice in my dream said something else, something I didn't
tell Annie. Nobody wants to hear bad news so I left that part
out, but I remember it word for word. You've done well,
Ophelia Browne, he said, but your time on earth is growing short.

*That's exactly what he said, and I don't doubt it's true. As I've told
you before, Browne family women seldom live past ninety. Edward told
me his Aunt Harriet lived to ninety-three, but she's the only one. Fact is
fact, and it makes no difference whether you're born into the Browne
family or marry into it.*

*The truth is I'm ready to go whenever the Lord calls me. I've been
waiting almost sixty years to see my Edward again, so it will be one heck
of a reunion. As it is I've been on this earth so long I've nearly worn out
my welcome.*

*They say every person has a purpose in life. At one time I thought my
purpose was being Edward's wife and the mother of his children, but as
you well know that wasn't to be. God knows how many years I've been
searching for another purpose and now when I'm almost out of time, I
finally find it.*

*It's Annie. She's my reason for being here. The dream made me see
that clear as day. Once she's on the road to happiness, then my work will
be done.*

*I know I told her one of my treasures is the key to her future, but I'm
not even sure of that. The truth is I don't have an answer. The voice
didn't say a word about what I had to do; it just said her destiny is in my*

hands. *So I started thinking about it, and the only thing I could figure out is that it's got to be the memory In one of my treasures. I don't have anything else of worth. If I did I'd surely give it to her.*

When you're short on years you don't have the luxury of stretching things out the way you do when you're young. It would have been nice if Annie and I could've spent years getting to know one another, but that's water under the bridge. She's here now, and that's all that counts.

I know I'm not really her mama, but in a strange way I feel like I am. I look into those violet eyes of hers and see myself seventy or eighty years ago. Having Annie with me is the closest I've ever come to having a daughter, so I'm determined to enjoy every minute we've got.

Tomorrow I'm going to start telling her about the memories I've found. All of them, right down to the tiniest one. She feels things the way I do, so I think when something important comes along she'll know it.

God knows I hope she does.

THE WATCH

On Saturday Annie spends most of the day trying to straighten the front wheel of the bicycle. After hearing Ophelia's prediction that a memory will change her life, she is more determined than ever to ride it. Although Ophelia has said it could be any one of many treasures, Annie is certain it is the bicycle.

She removes the wheel and lays it on the flat slab of sidewalk in front of the house. Now she can see exactly where the problem is. To the eye it looks small enough, but when it bumps against the fender the bicycle is impossible to steer. She first tries pushing it back into place, but the metal rim doesn't budge. Not even when she leans her full weight on it. When that fails, she takes a hammer from the shed and starts tapping the edge. At first it looks like she is making progress, but then she sees the bulge is simply moving from one spot to another.

Earlier in the week Annie searched the Internet for recommendations on how to fix a bicycle wheel. She found plenty of suggestions, but some were too complicated and others required tools she'd never before heard of. A few offered bits of information that might actually help.

Adjusting the spokes is what comes to mind. Trying to remember the instructions, she tightens the tension on one side of the wheel and loosens it on the opposite side. Once that is done she stands the wheel on its side and tries rolling it. It wobbles to the left and she can see the bump is larger. She again lays the wheel flat and reverses the action, tightening what she'd loosened and loosening what she'd tightened. The bump is now smaller than it was, but when she tries rolling the wheel it again wobbles. Less than before, but still falling to the left

With frustration picking at her brain and rivulets of sweat rolling down her back, Annie uses the last helpful tip she can remember. She lifts the wheel over her head and, with every bit of muscle she can muster, slams it down against the concrete. When she hears the snap of metal Annie covers her eyes, afraid to look. After several seconds she spreads her fingers and peers through the opening. It looks like the bump is gone, but that's what she thought last time. She flips the wheel over and finds the bump is not visible on that side either. She sets the wheel upright and rolls it. When the wheel goes straight, she leaps into the air and shouts for joy.

As soon as the bicycle is back together she calls for Ophelia to come and watch as she rides.

Annie climbs on the bike, pushes down on the pedal and off she goes.

"It works!" she screams, then disappears around a bend in the road.

Ophelia stands there smiling, and only after she has watched Annie circle the block twice does she uncross the fingers she's holding behind her back.

⊙══◆══⊙

Back in Philadelphia, Michael checks his cell phone for the seventeenth time and there is still no call from Annie.

"Ungrateful bitch," he mumbles.

Back and forth he paces. Back and forth, time and again. Sometimes he is teary-eyed, and other times he spits out words of anger and hatred.

When day turns to evening, he tells himself she is not worth his while. He dresses in a black shirt and trousers, then splashes a heavy layer of cologne on his neck. When he tromps out, he leaves his cell phone on the hall table.

"Screw her," he says. "Let her see what it feels like to be left waiting."

He is still confident Annie will call.

Down at the wharf he picks up a blonde from Cincinnati, and they go drinking. They drink martinis and she keeps up with him, matching drink for drink.

They are on their third round of drinks when she asks if he's married.

"Do I look married?" Michael answers.

She gives him a toothy smile and says, "No, but maybe you got a girlfriend you ain't telling me about."

"No girlfriend," Michael says. Then he slides his hand along the edge of her skirt.

Now that Annie has ridden the bicycle, she is confident she will soon come to know the boy. She has yet to hear the lad himself, but twice she has heard the sound of people calling his name. Both times the voices were far away and too muffled to make out distinctly. Still, she knows she is on the verge of finding him. When the wind whistles past her ears she pictures him riding in front of her. She can hear the puff of his breath. He is riding the same bicycle as she is, but his is newer, shinier. It is as if they are racing—she pedals fast trying to catch up, trying to grab a glimpse of his face. He pedals faster yet. Annie senses he is afraid of something, but she has no idea of what or who.

For the first time in many years Annie feels light as a feather. Her days are spent bicycling, gardening and listening to Ophelia's stories.

On Tuesday the weather turns to summer, and they have supper on the porch. After they eat, Ophelia pours two mugs of dandelion tea. She has begun to add two tablespoons of marigold to every pot because she believes it will enhance Annie's ability to feel the memories in each treasure. As they sip their tea, she pulls a gold pocket watch from the folds of her apron and lays it on the table. She waits to see if Annie will pick it up.

"How pretty," Annie says and lifts it into her hand.

Suddenly it is like the sting of a bee in her palm, and she gasps.

"Ow!"

She drops the watch back onto the table. Her expression is one of disbelief when she looks up. "Did you steal this?"

"Not me." Ophelia laughs. "But I believe it was at one time stolen."

"It stung my hand when I—"

Again Ophelia laughs. "I know. I felt the same sting the first time I picked it up. You have to hold it for a while before you can feel the good memories."

Annie lifts the watch again. This time there is no sting. The watch feels warm in her hand, but she feels nothing beyond that warmth.

For the remainder of the evening Annie keeps the watch folded in her hand.

"There are actually three watches like this," Ophelia explains. "Two of them were created as a replica of the first, which was stolen."

"How do you know that?" Annie asks.

"The watch told me," Ophelia replies.

"You knew it was a replica?"

"This isn't a replica," Ophelia says. "It's the original. A man named Wilbur carried that watch for fifty years, and his daddy carried it before him."

"Wilbur," Annie repeats. The name is a seed she is planting in her memory.

"Wilbur had three loves in his life," Ophelia says. "His first wife, then Ida and then—"

"Caroline," Annie says.

Ophelia's face is struck with amazement. "How did you—"

Annie doesn't wait for the rest of the question. "I don't know. I didn't even realize I was going to say something. My mouth just opened and out it came."

A smile of satisfaction curls Ophelia's lips. "Good. It proves you can do it." She explains how she carried the watch for weeks before she could catch the memory of Wilbur's story, and then it came only after she began sleeping with the watch tucked beneath her pillow.

When the moon is high in the sky, Ophelia yawns and says it is time for bed. She hands Annie the watch.

"Sleep with it beneath your pillow," she says. "Perhaps you will find more about the memory in a dream."

That night Annie is awakened by the smell of smoke, and she can feel the heat of nearby flames. Her first thought is of Ophelia. Barefoot and in her pajamas, she dashes up the stairs. With three long strides she crosses to Ophelia's bed.

"Wake up! Wake up!" she screams, tugging at the old woman's shoulder.

Ophelia is sound asleep, and it is several seconds before she opens her eyes.

"Quick, we've got to get out of here!" Annie shouts. "The house is on fire!"

Still struggling to come fully awake, Ophelia asks, "What are you talking about? There's no fire."

"Yes, there is!" She pulls back the comforter and reaches for Ophelia's arm. "Can't you smell the…" Suddenly Annie realizes she no longer smells the smoke.

"Wait here," she tells Ophelia and goes to investigate. She descends the stairs slowly, stopping on each step and sniffing at the air. There is no trace of smoke, no flame, no hint of there ever being a fire. Room by room she searches the house, stepping out onto the porch, looking across to the garden and beyond the willow. Everything is as still and peaceful as it was when she went to bed.

Annie is certain there was smoke and flames, but now there is nothing. Returning to the loft she apologizes to Ophelia for such a foolish mistake.

"I can't imagine why I thought…"

After she is back in her own bed it is a long while before she falls asleep. The fright of the fire is still with her, and it causes her heart to beat like the rat-tat-tat of a snare drum. There is no thought of the watch beneath her pillow.

THE REALITY OF REGRET

For the first three days Michael tells himself Annie can go to hell as far as he is concerned. He is certain she wants him to come crawling on his hands and knees begging for her forgiveness. He is equally certain that he'll never do it.

"We'll see who can wait the longest," he says. Yet he checks the messages on his cell phone several times an hour.

In the week she has been gone he has slept with two different women. Both times were disastrous. Instead of enjoying his flings he found himself thinking about Annie and became as impotent as a baby.

It seems as though the week has been a month long, and when Wednesday turns into Thursday with no call he starts to worry. Tomorrow will be Friday, and he thinks Annie just might leave town to spend another weekend with her so-called friend.

Enough is enough. He is not ready to struggle through another weekend of waiting for her to call, but he is also not willing to go in waving the white flag of surrender.

On Thursday morning he decides to stop by her office and casually invite her to lunch. Not a date, just lunch. He'll make it sound like sort of a friendship thing. He'll mention that he was looking for his blue jacket and thinks he might have left it at her apartment. She's bound to mention the flowers, and after she does he'll ask if she wants to grab a burger together. That should be enough to get the ball rolling.

When he arrives at Metropolitan Underwriting at ten-thirty Thursday morning, he is already planning their weekend together. Saturday night it will be dinner at Jean Pierre, and on Sunday they can take in a Phillies game.

He has been to her office a number of times before, so Michael doesn't bother to stop at the receptionist's desk; he breezes by and heads for where he knows he will find Annie. When he rounds the corner, Peter is sitting at Annie's desk.

"Shit," he mumbles. As he crosses to the desk, he forces a smile to his face then casually asks, "Is Annie around?"

Peter is surprised to see Michael here but even more surprised by the question.

"No," he answers. "She hasn't been here since last Friday."

"Last Friday?"

Peter nods. "Didn't she tell you?"

Visibly annoyed, Michael asks, "Tell me what?"

"Annie quit her job on Friday; she hasn't been back since."

Michael is not only bewildered, he is also embarrassed. He has been made to look a fool, and that's something that rankles him down to the soles of his feet.

"Oh, right," he says. "I've been out of town and forgot about her mentioning that she planned to quit." He turns to leave.

"She planned to quit?" Peter asks.

"Yeah," Michael replies. "Apparently there was some brouhaha about not getting the promotion she wanted. You know how women are."

Peter doesn't bother to answer. He knows Michael is lying. Once Michael disappears down the hallway, Peter dials Annie's home number and leaves a message.

"This is Peter," he says. "Call me."

When Michael leaves Metropolitan Underwriting, he heads for Annie's apartment building. Joe Felder is the doorman on duty when he scuttles by. He gives Joe a quick wave and disappears into the elevator.

In front of Annie's apartment is the bouquet of roses. They are limp, and many of the flowers have already turned brown. He rings the doorbell several times and then reaches for the ledge above the door. There is no key.

For several minutes Michael stands in front of the door. He is dumbfounded at this turn of events. When there is no other alternative, he returns to the lobby and tells Joe he's again forgotten his key to the apartment.

"Can you let me in?" he asks.

"No problem," Joe says and pulls a ring of master keys from his desk.

As they ride up in the elevator Michael makes small talk and tries to sound casual, but his heart pounds against his chest and he hopes the nervous twitch in his right eye is not noticeable.

As they step from the elevator, Joe asks, "You and the missus been away?"

"Sort of," Michael answers. He claims Annie has a sick friend she's visiting, and he's been traveling for business.

Joe gives a nod, "Thought so, since I ain't seen either of you around all week." He unlocks the door and pushes it open.

"Thanks," Michael says and folds a ten-dollar bill into Joe's hand.

Once Joe is gone Michael rummages through the apartment, not sure what he is looking for but hoping to find an indication of Annie's whereabouts. She has never before done anything this rash, and he is at a loss to understand why she would do it now. As drawer after drawer reveals nothing, Michael grows increasingly more worried. Okay, they had an argument, but surely she knew he'd be back. He always came back.

When he finishes searching the apartment and finds nothing, he plops down on the sofa. None of this makes sense, he tells himself. Her clothes are still hanging in the closet, so she's obviously planning to come back. But when? And from where?

As Michael sits and thinks back on the seven years they spent together, he realizes he doesn't want to lose Annie. It's the marriage thing that's the problem, he decides. That's the only thing it could be. Other than arguments about marriage and kids, they were okay together. They always had fun. She was right for him, and whether or not she realizes it he was right for her.

Although it is early in the afternoon, Michael pulls a bottle of scotch from the cabinet and pours himself a drink. He takes one sip then sits there holding it in his hand. The thought of losing Annie is terrifying. Even during the months they'd been separated, he always believed he could come back whenever he wanted to. He knew she'd be there. Now, he's not so sure.

Before Michael leaves the apartment, he takes the spare key Annie keeps in the kitchen drawer and tucks it into his wallet. He needs assurance that he will be able to get into the apartment again. Once he is face to face with her she'll have to listen. He's certain that when she hears what he's got to say, any issues standing between them will be resolved. But first he needs to find her.

He pulls a fifty-dollar bill from his wallet then stops at the lobby desk. Sliding the bill into Joe's hand he says, "Annie and I had a bit of an argument, and you know how women are. I think she's staying away to spite me. I can't sit here and wait, but if you could give me a call as soon as she gets back…"

Joe glances down at the bill in his hand and sees Ulysses S. Grant smiling back.

"Sure, Mister Stavros," he says, "I'll be happy to call."

Joe Felder suspects there is more to the story than Michael has suggested, but his wife's birthday is next week and with fifty bucks he can take her out to dinner at a nice restaurant.

THE BALL

When Annie wakes the next morning it is drizzling rain, and for a few minutes she remains in bed. This is when she remembers the pocket watch beneath her pillow. She raises herself to a sitting position, reaches beneath the pillow and fishes the watch from its resting place. Covering the face of the watch is a thin layer of black soot, the residue of a fire. It wasn't there last night, of that Annie is certain. For several minutes she remains there holding the watch in the palm of her hand. She vividly remembers the smell of smoke and the heat of fire. She can even recall the fear that gripped her heart.

Slowly Annie peels open these recollections and comes to the realization that she has moved past finding good memories in the things left behind. She is able to feel the bad memories as well.

When they sit down to breakfast, she shows Ophelia the watch and shares the story.

"I could feel the fire," she says, "but I never saw the Wilbur you spoke of. It felt as though the thoughts were mine and someone I loved was in danger." Annie stirs a spoonful of honey into her tea and then continues. "I'm sure that wasn't Wilbur's memory. I think it was the girl Caroline's memory of him."

Although she believes this is true, Annie can't explain how she knows it. She knows only that there is more to the story, other events that came before and after. A feeling of apprehension settles in her heart. As much as she wants to find the missing pieces, she is frightened of what she might discover.

"Is it possible that a memory can come to life and happen again?"

When Annie asks this question, there is a quiver in her voice.

"I don't believe so," Ophelia answers. She sees the look of concern wrinkling Annie's forehead and adds, "But perhaps it would be best to set the watch aside for now."

This is a new experience for Ophelia; she has sensed only good memories and the occasional black hole that hid any unpleasantry. She is uncertain how to handle it or if in fact it is opening the door to a yet unknown danger. She has never known a memory to leave its resting place and come to life, but perhaps the girl's power is far greater than her own. She takes the watch from Annie's hand and slides it into her pocket. If there is an evil memory in the watch, she does not want Annie to touch upon it.

"Some memories are better off left to the past," she says.

Outside the day is grey and gloomy. The weeping willow casts a dark shadow across the lawn and an occasional gust of wind whips leaves from the tree, making them fall as if they are cascading teardrops. Searching her mind for an object that will move Annie's thoughts away from the watch, she remembers the ball.

When breakfast is finished Annie clears the table, and Ophelia makes her way up the staircase to the loft. She returns with the boy's ball in her pocket. It is too damp to sit on the porch today, so they settle in the front parlor.

Ophelia sits on the sofa and pulls the woolen throw over her legs. Although the heat of summer is fast approaching, she is chilled and welcomes the warmth. Annie comes and tucks the blanket close around her knees.

"Is that comfy?" she asks.

Ophelia replies that it is; then she pulls the ball from her pocket and hands it to Annie.

"I thought since we're stuck inside today you might want take another look at this," she says.

Annie gives a broad smile, then sits in the rocker closest to the sofa. She is not anxious to know more about the fiery watch, but the thought of knowing more about the bicycle boy thrills her. She takes the ball in her hand and runs her fingers across the bite marks. The spacing tells her the dog was neither large nor small.

With the ball cradled in both hands, she closes her eyes and sees the brown dog running beside the boy on a bicycle. Her view is still from the back, so she knows nothing more than she did before.

Annie opens her eyes and absently throws the ball against the opposite wall. She is lost in thought as she does this. The ball thunks against the wall then bounces off the floor and back to her. Three times she does it...thunk, bounce, thunk, bounce.

The third bounce is just inches away from the milk glass lamp that once belonged to Edward's mother.

"I don't think you should be doing that," Ophelia says. "You're liable to break something."

Suddenly Annie shouts, "Ethan Allen!"

She catches the ball and holds it in her hands. "I heard his name. It sounded like you talking, but it wasn't you." She hesitates a moment then adds, "It was the woman who takes care of him."

"His mother?" Ophelia asks.

Annie shakes her head. "Not his mother. His grandma maybe."

"So the lad's name is Ethan Allen?" Ophelia gives a nod of satisfaction and says, "I didn't give you that memory; you found it on your own."

Annie smiles and pockets the ball.

The rain continues, sometimes heavy, sometimes little more than a drizzle, but it is enough to keep them inside. They spend the entire afternoon sitting in the parlor. Given the gloom of the day, Ophelia focuses on telling the happy stories of her life with Edward. She describes a vacation they took to Virginia Beach and tells how they splashed in the ocean and ran barefoot in the sand.

"There were flocks of tiny sandpipers," she says with a laugh, "and when the waves washed out they would dart into the wet sand, peck around for bits of food and then scurry off before another wave rolled in."

When Ophelia speaks of Edward, her eyes appear lit from within. The sallow color of her skin grows flushed with pink, and the sound of her laughter becomes that of a young girl.

"As lovely as the days were," she says, "the evenings were my favorite time. After dinner we would go dancing in the hotel ballroom." She stops in the middle of her story and explains that back in those days most hotels had ballrooms with a live band playing dance music. With a tinge of sadness in her voice she says, "There have been so many changes in the world; I doubt people have time for dancing now."

"True." Annie nods. "Michael and I hardly ever went dancing, and when we did we stepped all over each other's feet."

"Edward and I never had that problem," Ophelia replies. "The very first time he took me in his arms, we moved as if we were one person." The memory of this is obvious on her face when she adds, "His arms were so strong, when he held me my feet barely touched the floor."

All afternoon they sit and talk. Annie continues to cradle the ball in her hands; she wishes another memory would come. When she goes to the kitchen to prepare a light lunch of tea and buttered biscuits, she brings the ball with her.

When Annie carries the lunch tray into the parlor she pours two mugs of tea. In the time she was gone Ophelia's color has grown sallow again.

"Are you feeling okay?" Annie asks as she hands Ophelia the mug,

Ophelia nods. "Yes," she answers, but Annie can see there is something more. Something Ophelia does not care to talk about.

That night supper is later than usual, and instead of a pleasant meal on the side porch they eat in the kitchen with the sound of rain hammering against the window. The melancholic sound deepens the lines in Ophelia's face.

When they have finished eating, the table cleared and the supper dishes put away, Ophelia says she is ready for bed. "Rainy days are trying on the soul," she claims.

Still clinging to the ball and eager for more, Annie asks if she can sleep with it under her pillow. She hopes to dream of the boy. Despite the vivid memory of last night's fire, she still feels certain it is the boy who will change her life.

Although Ophelia nods her approval, she has a growing fear that Annie will discover things she has no knowledge of. Memories intended to remain secret.

Before she climbs into bed Annie carefully tucks the ball beneath her pillow. As she closes her eyes she thinks of the boy. She pictures him riding the bicycle. It is the last thought she has before sleep overcomes her.

That night there are no dreams, good or bad. There is only the constant splash of rain against the window and an occasional squawk from the ducks on the pond. Several times during the night she wakes and glances at the clock on the nightstand. She wants it to be morning, but the hands of time are stuck in the wee hours that cross from night into day. When the first ray of dawn finally lights the horizon she pulls herself from the bed and stumbles into the kitchen.

Ophelia is not yet downstairs, so Annie brews a pot of tea and mixes the batter for banana pancakes. In the weeks she has been here she has grown familiar with where everything is. She could make her way around the kitchen and, for that matter, the entire house blindfolded—with perhaps the single exception of the loft. Annie has visited Ophelia in the loft, but she has not yet grasped the feel of it.

The loft belongs to Ophelia. It is, in itself, her greatest treasure. It holds the memories that are hers alone. The secrets of the loft are not Annie's to take; she cannot picture Edward laughing or dancing. She sees him only as he appears in the photograph on Ophelia's nightstand.

OPHELIA

*W*hen heartache settles into your soul you want to believe
that in time it will pass. You tell yourself, This is the misery
I must live with now, but one day it will be less painful. The
sorry truth is some heartaches never lessen. The sound of rain still
brings back the memory of Edward's death.

It was raining the day I returned from visiting Mama. Not just a
drizzle; a real downpour. I remember hoping Edward had thought to
bring an umbrella. When I climbed down from the train and saw he
wasn't waiting, let me tell you, I was pretty piqued. But after an hour had
ticked by I knew something terrible was wrong. It wasn't like Edward to
be late and even less likely he'd forget I was coming on the afternoon
train.

There was no overhang at the old rail station, but that didn't stop
me. I stood out there in the pouring rain until the next taxi cab came by,
then I jumped in and told him the address of where to go. That's out of
my district, he said. I leaned forward so far my face was up next to his. I
don't care a fig about what's in or out of your district, I told him, you get
me home right this minute. He charged me double because he had to
drive out there and then back again, but I didn't argue about that. I was
too worried about Edward to be thinking of money.

When I got out of the cab and ran to the front door, it was locked. I
had to poke around in my bag to find the key. By the time I got inside I
was soaked through. I still remember the smell of those wet clothes and
the way the rainwater dripped down my leg and puddled on the floor.

Lord God, that was an awful time. A little thunderstorm doesn't bother me, but when we have downpours like we did yesterday it brings the misery back.

You might wonder why I didn't say what was bothering me when Annie asked; it's because heartache isn't a thing to be passed around. Everyone gets their share of heartaches in life, and piling your share on somebody else's plate isn't what the Lord intended.

I've lived with the sorrow of that day all these years, so I suppose I can keep it to myself for a short while longer.

IN THE MONTHS THAT FOLLOW

Throughout the summer Annie remains at Memory House. She no longer dwells on thoughts of Michael; her days are filled with gardening and her evenings spent listening to the magical tales Ophelia shares.

There is a quilt with a scattering of stars on a field of blue. This, Ophelia explains, was made by a woman celebrating life, but exactly why she cannot say. She knows only that the stars represent friends. The oversized yellow patch is a moon showing the fullness of life, and the tree with its roots winding along the edges of the quilt is the anchor that holds everything in place.

"This woman is happy," Ophelia says. "Very happy. See." She points to the tiny stiches running along the tendrils of the roots. "Every stitch is small and even. Only a contented heart has the patience to do that."

Annie would like to know more, but there is nothing more to be told. Ophelia catches only small glimpses of other lives, memories that are there one moment and gone the next.

It is the same with the Christmas ornament, a ball that pops open and exposes a red satin lining.

"This once held a ring and a promise," Ophelia says, but like the quilt she knows only of that moment. She can feel the happiness in the memory but knows nothing of the person it belongs to.

Annie touches her fingers to each new item, trying to see more than Ophelia has spoken of, but the quilt is simply a cloth in her hand. And the ornament, charming though it may be, tells nothing.

As she listens Annie thinks back on Ophelia's words. "One of my treasures will change your life." With each new unveiling she tries to will a memory to surface.

They are sitting on the side porch when Ophelia pulls a silver locket from the pocket of her apron. It is late in the afternoon, and the sun is low in the sky. As the locket dangles from her fingers, a flicker of the setting sun dances across it and for one split second there is a glint that seems bright as the flash from a camera.

Before Ophelia has spoken, Annie reaches for the locket. She has seen the flash as a sign.

Handing over the locket, Ophelia says, "Look inside."

Annie pops open the heart-shaped locket. Inside there is a faded photograph of a black man. Although she can see little more than his face, she knows he is a farmer.

"Who is he?" she asks.

Ophelia shrugs. "I don't know. I only know he gave this to a woman named Delia. The night he first clasped it around her neck, they were in a place where you could smell the earth and fresh-cut grass."

Annie folds her fingers around the locket and holds it to her heart. She is expecting to feel what Ophelia has felt. At first there is nothing; then the locket grows warm in her hand.

"The day I found that locket, I knew it was a treasure," Ophelia says. "I can't say how I knew, I just knew. For weeks I slept with it under my pillow and then on a night when the moon was so full and bright it lit the loft, the dream came to me."

She explains how she saw the two of them together, Delia just a mere slip of a girl but with the light of love shining in her face.

"When I woke I remembered the words he'd spoken."

Still clutching the locket to her heart, Annie leans in and asks, "What were they?"

Repeating the words just as she remembers, Ophelia replies, "Delia, I love you with all my heart, and if you're willing to have me I'd like to marry you."

"What did Delia say?" Annie asks.

"I never heard her words," Ophelia answers. "But I have to believe she said yes, because I could see them making love."

Annie laughs. "You actually saw them making love?"

Ophelia chuckles. "Not the way you're thinking. It was a blurry picture, like they have in the movies."

When Ophelia gives her approval, Annie clasps the locket around her own neck. She is convinced that, like the bicycle and the ball, it will eventually let go of a memory.

All summer she wears the locket. It has the look and feel of something with a secret to share, and she is determined to find it. When she sits idle, Annie fingers the locket and thinks back on the words of Ophelia's story. Eventually she can picture the couple, not close up but from a distance. She sees them sitting in the grass and feels the sweetness of their kiss. As time passes this picture settles in her head, but she no longer knows whether she has actually gathered this memory or it's merely a version of the story she has heard.

In the months she has been here, Annie has learned to mix potions as Ophelia does and, like her mentor, she spins tales of encouragement and hope.

"A pretty girl like you doesn't need a potion to cause a man to fall in love," she tells Sara Jean Lewes as she hands her a mix of lemon verbena and jasmine.

Sara Jean smiles. Like many of the other customers, she finds it easy to talk to Annie. So the word passes from one customer to the next, and it is said that Annie is a younger version of Ophelia.

"I remember when Ophelia was that age," Eldridge Mercer says, "and she was the spitting image of Annie."

It is nearing the end of August when Annie tells Ophelia that she must return to Philadelphia.

"I've got to get the rest of my things and find someone to sublet the apartment," she says.

A cloud crosses Ophelia's face. "You will come back, won't you?"

"Of course," Annie answers. Her words are sincere for there is no doubt in her mind that she will return. With fall coming there will be less work to do in the garden, but she is ready to go in search of a job. She will need the suits and dresses left hanging in the closet.

"I should be back within a week," she promises.

Before she leaves, Annie calls three of the customers who frequent the apothecary.

"I'll be away for a week," she tells them and asks if they could look in on Ophelia.

"She's perfectly fine," Annie explains. "It's just that she had that one fainting spell…"

It is the Tuesday after Labor Day when Annie kisses Ophelia goodbye and leaves for Philadelphia. She is still wearing the heart-shaped locket.

PHILADELPHIA

The traffic is light and the drive easy, so Annie is back at her apartment building before four o'clock. Albert Cannelli is the doorman on duty. Annie stops at the reception desk and asks for the mail they have been holding.

Albert hands her a hefty pack of envelopes held together by a rubber band.

"Good to have you back," he says.

Annie smiles. "I won't be here long. I'm moving to Virginia."

"Mister Stavros going too?" he asks.

Annie shakes her head. "We're not together anymore. It's just me."

He is now interested. "What about the apartment?"

"I've yet to figure that out," Annie replies. "I'm thinking maybe sublet."

"You know Marjorie Prescott? Lives down the block at the Concord?"

Annie is familiar with the Concord. It is a larger building with wrap-around terraces and rents that are twice what she pays.

"Afraid not," she answers.

"Her husband passed away a few months back," Albert says. "I think she's looking for a smaller place. If you want I could make a phone call."

"That would be great," Annie replies.

As she turns and disappears into the elevator, Albert smiles. He is thinking about the twenty bucks he'll collect when he tells Marjorie Prescott he's found her an apartment at Remington Arms.

When Joe Felder comes on duty at seven o'clock, he asks Albert if anything is new. Albert shakes his head.

"Nothing worth talking about," he says, making no mention of Annie's return or the fact that she will be moving out.

Once Albert is gone, Joe settles in behind the desk, grabs the *Philadelphia Inquirer* and turns to the Sports section. It's the end of the season, and he's looking to see how the Phillies did in last night's game. There is almost no chance they'll make the playoffs, which for Joe is a big disappointment, especially since they have a new right fielder.

When he's finished with the Sports section Joe moves on to the local news and then the national news. From time to time he looks up and nods at one of the residents coming or going, but it is an otherwise quiet evening; that is, until Martin Selznick comes to the desk saying he's locked himself out of his apartment.

"I went to drop some trash down the incinerator," Selznick says, "and the door slammed shut."

Joe pulls open the storage drawer on the right side of the reception console and reaches for the ring of master keys, but in doing so he notices that the fat packet of mail they'd been holding for Annie Cross is gone.

"What the..." he grumbles. While Selznick is still standing there waiting to be let back into his apartment, Joe rummages through all of the other drawers thinking perhaps the mail has been misplaced or moved.

Joe searches through first one drawer and then the other, but Selznick, a man with a short fuse to begin with, grows impatient.

"What's taking so long?" he asks.

"Just trying to make sure I've got the right key," Joe answers. He pushes the drawer shut, flips the reception desk answering machine on and follows Martin Selznick to the elevator.

Once the door is unlocked and he is rid of Selznick, Joe heads for Annie's apartment. He stops outside her door and listens. At first he hears nothing, but then he catches the sound of someone moving around inside the apartment. He waits for several minutes, and while there are more sounds of movement there is no voice so he is uncertain if this is Annie or Michael.

He returns to the reception desk and pushes the call button for apartment 5C. It is only a few moments before he hears Annie's voice.

"Yes?" she says.

"Oops," Joe replies, "sorry, Missus Stavros, I hit the wrong intercom button."

"No problem," Annie replies and clicks off.

Seconds later Joe picks up the phone and dials the number on the card he's been carrying in his wallet. When Michael answers, Joe says, "Missus Stavros is back in the building."

"Thanks," Michael says and hangs up.

It is after eleven when he arrives at Remington Arms. When the call came Michael was sitting in an armchair wearing boxer shorts and a tee shirt; now he is dressed in the blue suit Annie always admired. He is carrying a bouquet of yellow roses, and there is an unfamiliar bulge in the pocket of his jacket.

As he crosses the lobby he grins and gives Joe a thumbs-up.

Stepping into the elevator Michael presses the button for the fifth floor, but as the doors whoosh open he begins to wonder if it is better to ring the doorbell or just walk in and surprise her.

Standing behind the protection of a closed door Annie could easily as not tell him to go away, but Michael is confident that once she sees the flowers and hears what he has to say the past will be forgotten. He decides to use the key in his wallet.

Making every effort to be as noiseless as possible, he slides the key into the lock and turns the tumbler.

THE QUESTION

Annie is in the kitchen when she hears the click. Before she has time to get to the phone in the bedroom, the door opens and she hears the squeak of the hinge. She is alone. Her cell phone is in her purse, the purse on the living room coffee table. Grabbing hold of the bread knife on the counter, she holds it close to her chest and presses herself against the wall.

From the living room Annie is invisible. She makes no sound, but the pounding of her heart thunders in her ears. She prays that the intruder can neither see nor hear her, that he will be content to grab the purse and run.

The door closes, and there are footsteps in the hall.

Michael walks into the living room. He sees the purse on the coffee table and knows Annie is there. He turns toward the bedroom, glances around and then turns back.

To Annie it seems like an hour has passed, but in actuality it has been less than a minute. She is holding her breath when Michael calls out her name.

Recognizing his voice, she steps from behind the wall brandishing the knife.

"Michael, what in the name of God are you doing here?" A rush of relief swooshes through her; then her voice grows angry. "Are you crazy? You're lucky I didn't stab you!"

This is not what Michael expects, and he is momentarily at a loss for words. "We've made a mistake," he stammers.

"*You've* made a mistake," Annie says. "A big mistake. What makes you think you can just walk into my apartment any time you want?"

"I thought it was *our* apartment," Michael answers cynically. It is too late for a game of guessing what he has for her. He pulls the yellow roses from behind his back and holds them out.

"Well, it's not our apartment," Annie snaps. It is as if she hasn't seen the flowers. "It stopped being our apartment when you moved out."

"That was a mistake," he says. "I realize it now."

Annie turns away. This is something she doesn't want to hear. With her back to Michael she carries the knife to the kitchen. This movement gives her time to think.

"No, it wasn't a mistake," she finally says. "We were never right for each other."

He drops the roses onto the table and crosses the room, approaching her from the back. With his hands on her shoulders he swings her around so they are face-to-face and mere inches apart.

"We were always meant to be together," he says. "It's just that I didn't realize it until now." There is a strange earnestness in his words, and it touches Annie's heart.

The anger in her face softens. "Don't say that. We've been down this road before, and it's not good for either one of us."

With his hands still on her shoulders Michael tries to ease her into an embrace, but she is stiff and unyielding.

"You're wrong," he says. "I want you back, Annie, and I'm willing to change. I'll do whatever it takes to make it work."

The kitchen is small, and suddenly the intensity of his closeness unnerves her. Annie wrenches herself from his grip and turns toward the living room.

He follows close behind. "I'm in love with you, Annie. Why can't you see that?"

She stops and turns to face him. "You might think you're in love with me, but it's not the same as loving me. In-love is short-term. It only lasts until the thrill is gone. Loving someone lasts forever."

"I want it to be forever." He reaches into his pocket and pulls out a blue velvet box. "This will prove it." He pushes back the top of the box and holds out a diamond engagement ring.

Annie makes no move to accept it.

"Don't you get it?" he says. His voice is now louder and more demanding. "I'm asking you to marry me!"

She lowers her eyes so that she is no longer looking into his face. "I'm sorry, I can't." Annie tries to explain that she no longer loves him, but before she can get the words out he grabs her by the arms and shakes her. Hard.

"Can't?!" he screams. "What the hell is that supposed to mean? For years you've been after me to get married—"

"Things were different then. I'm sorry—"

"Sorry? What kind of shit is sorry?" He pushes her away and starts pacing back and forth. "All these years you've been at me. Marry me, marry me, marry me. Then when I give you what you want, you say sorry. Is this your sick idea of payback?"

Annie tries to stay calm, but inside her chest there is a rumbling of fear. "At the time I was sincere, but things have changed."

Michael stops and stares at her with a heavy-eyed look. "Changed?"

Annie nods. "I've learned that love goes way beyond what we had. Loving someone is about giving, not taking."

"That's a load of bullshit!" Michael shouts. "There's no old lady friend, is there? It's some guy, isn't it?"

When he starts toward her, Annie backs away.

"Is this what it's all about?" He reaches out and yanks the heart-shaped locket from her neck.

The thin silver chain snaps easily, but when it does Annie feels something slam against her body. She falls backward, hits her head against the bookcase and drops to the floor.

When she comes to Michael is leaning over her with an icy cold cloth.

"I'm sorry," he says. "I saw the locket and thought…"

"There is nobody else," Annie says.

"Then why?"

"Because I realize that by marrying you I'd just be filling the empty hole in my life. I want someone who will be the whole of my life."

"That doesn't make sense. What's filling a hole supposed to mean?"

"It means not having to go to bed alone, not having to wonder who you'll spend New Year's Eve and Valentine's Day with. It's settling for an okay relationship instead of waiting for something spectacular."

Michael drops to the floor and sits alongside Annie. He takes her hand in his. "I thought we were good together."

"We were," Annie replies. "But that was a long time ago."

As they sit together and talk of what once was, Michael's tone slowly changes from anger to regret and ultimately to acceptance. Anger and bitterness are replaced by sadness, but there is no turning back. When he finally stands to leave, it is almost one o'clock.

He reaches into his pocket, pulls out the key he used and hands it to Annie. "I guess I won't be needing this anymore."

⊙▬◆▬⊙

That same night Annie takes the silver locket and puts it in a box. She will never wear it again. Tucking the small white box into her suitcase, Annie prays this is not the treasure destined to change her life.

ANNIE

*T*hat was the scariest thing I've ever experienced. When Michael tore the locket off my neck, it felt like someone hit me in the back with a baseball bat. It wasn't Michael. He can be ill tempered and nasty, but he'd never do something like that.

I have to believe it was a memory or maybe part of a memory that belonged to the woman who wore the locket. Delia. I thought I heard her scream just as the pain hit, but then I blacked out. I don't know why I thought it was her, I just did.

When I opened my eyes my brain was so fuzzy I couldn't think of where or even who I was. I saw a face leaning over me, but at first it looked like that black man whose picture is in the locket.

I didn't realize it was Michael until I heard his voice. He sounded almost as frightened as I was. I know he thinks he did it, but, honestly, it wasn't him. It was something way worse and way meaner than Michael.

I have no way of knowing what memory is attached to the locket but I can tell you this: it's not good. Something happened to that woman. Something too terrible to even imagine.

I'm not going to tell Ophelia about this; it would only worry her. She hasn't been feeling that well, and she's got her own concerns. If she wants to believe there's only good memories attached to the locket, then so be it.

Tomorrow I'll buy a new chain and she'll never be any the wiser. But after what happened tonight I promise you I'll never, ever wear that locket again. And I'm not going to let Ophelia wear it either.

Whatever secret it's carrying is better off forgotten.

THE LOCKET

By the end of the week Annie has packed everything she wants to take and sold those things she no longer needs. On the fifteenth of September Marjorie Prescott will take over the apartment, subletting it for the last year of the lease.

Saturday morning the young couple who bought the bedroom set come to carry it away. It is the last of the furnishings to go. Tomorrow morning Annie herself will be gone and the apartment will be empty of everything—her, Michael and the memories they've made.

She can't help but wonder if any of the things she is leaving behind has memories attached to them. Will the young couple one day discover the laughter she and Michael once shared, or will they find the sadness of the sleepless nights that followed? It is a question with no answer.

Until a few short months ago Annie believed memories were something that belonged only to oneself; now even that is a question. At times she is certain she has felt the impact of a memory, and yet the logic of it makes no sense. Nothing is fact. Everything is feeling.

Annie cleans the apartment one last time, then snuggles into a sleeping bag that will go with her tomorrow morning. It is a reminder of the weekend she and Michael went camping but it is, like Ophelia said, a feathered hat that contains no special memories.

⊙━━✦━━⊙

Daylight is just beginning to cross the horizon when Annie leaves

Philadelphia. Before two o'clock she is back in Burnsville, and Ophelia welcomes her with open arms. It is a new beginning for them. Annie is no longer a guest at Memory House; she is now part of Ophelia's world.

For the first week there is only the chores of unpacking the car and settling in. Annie has brought all of her personal belongings: books, memorabilia, pictures and the clothes she will need for finding a job. The room that once boasted a spacious closet and a dresser with empty drawers is now full to overflowing, but she has found a place for everything. Without sacrifice she has somehow whittled her life down from a good-sized apartment to a single room with a window that overlooks the pond. Nothing of meaning has been left behind. Even the blue ribbon she won in the ninth grade has made the trip.

Annie has kept the locket. It is tucked in the far back of a drawer packed with woolen sweaters. Unable to forget what happened, she promises herself she will not speak of it. But she does.

It happens seven days after her return, on a night with the lingering heat of summer and the stillness of a dead person. They have settled on the side porch with tall glasses of iced tea and a plate of raspberry cookies when Ophelia notices she is no longer wearing the locket and asks about it.

For a moment Annie stumbles over her words; they are uncomfortable and clumsy. It is the first time she has told an outright lie to Ophelia, and it does not come easily. She claims that since she has not yet gathered memories from the locket she has placed it under her pillow to encourage a dream.

"Really?" Ophelia says. The look of doubt tugs at her face.

Annie can tell the lie has been seen through. "What I mean is that I didn't learn anything more about Delia or the man who gave it to her."

That answer is not enough for Ophelia. "Did something unusual, something out of the ordinary, happen while you were in Philadelphia?"

"There was the incident with Michael," Annie says, "but I've already told you about that."

Annie tries to edge away from the subject, but Ophelia persists. After almost six decades of peering into the thoughts of other people, she knows there is more. Something left unsaid.

"I wasn't referring to Michael," she says. "Did you find anything in the locket? Not just the words of Delia or the man she was with, anything?"

"I believe so," Annie finally answers. This is when she tells Ophelia of the blow she felt when the locket was torn from her neck.

"The pain was excruciating," she says, "so bad I blacked out. When I came to it wasn't there anymore. I could remember the pain, but I didn't know what caused it."

This is the first Ophelia has heard of a memory reaching out to touch someone. The thought is terrifying. "You're sure Michael didn't hit you?"

Annie gives a solemn nod. "I'm sure."

"Is it possible you fell and hit your back?"

"No," Annie answers. "Something hit me, and whatever it was came from a memory in the locket. I'm almost certain of it."

As she listens to the story Ophelia's face is a mask of worry, and her eyes darken to the color of cinder. "I want you to give the locket back to me," she says. Her words are pointed and purposeful.

"That's not a good idea," Annie answers. Although she acknowledges the locket belongs to Ophelia, she is fearful of the evil inside of it. "What if this happens again?"

Annie leaves the remainder of her thought unsaid, but she is thinking Ophelia's frail bones could not withstand the force of such a blow.

"Nothing will happen," Ophelia replies. "I've had the locket for a long time and not once have I had a problem. There's no reason why now…" She turns it off as if it is not a matter of concern, but the truth is she fears Annie has somehow unleashed a Pandora's box of memories.

It is the first time they argue about anything, but in the end Annie takes the locket from its hiding place and hands it back.

Treating it with casual irreverence, Ophelia drops it into her pocket and moves on to talking about her need for a new apple corer.

They sit together for another half hour; then Ophelia says she is tired and ready for bed. It is not yet ten o'clock when she leaves Annie at the table and goes to the loft.

Once upstairs, she sits in the small chair and listens for Annie's movements as an owl listens for a mouse to rustle through the leaves. It is almost an hour before she hears the girl go to her room and yet another hour before she hears the soft breaths of sleep. She waits a while longer to be certain, then starts down the stairs.

With her hand tightly gripping the banister Ophelia inches her way down with uncertain steps. There is only the light of the moon, so she moves slowly. After each step she stretches her toe down and finds the next tread before she continues. At the bottom of the staircase there is a light switch, but she passes it by and feels her way toward the front door.

Halfway across the room she bumps into the sofa and stops. She has taken a wrong turn. Hand over hand she moves along the back of the sofa until she comes to an open space that she knows is directly in front of the center hall. Careful not to topple the three-legged table she moves along the wall and feels for the doorframe, then turns the lock, twists the doorknob and steps outside.

Once she is outside the moonlight is brighter. She can see the flagstones of the walkway that leads to the pond. Keeping to the path she has trod for all these years, she circles the house and finds the grassy area beside the pond. Here she moves more slowly. At night the pond seems black, and the definition between water and land is blurred. Ophelia wishes she had brought a cane to steady her step and feel for what is ahead, but she hasn't and now it's too late.

When she nears the pond she can smell the water and hear the movement of fish. Still she moves forward. Only after she can feel the cold water swishing around her ankles does she take the two small objects in her hand and heave them into the center of the pond. There is a small splash and then another. After that there is nothing.

"That's it," she murmurs and steps from the water back onto the grass.

The moon is high in the sky and half the night is gone when Ophelia climbs into her bed. Her body is weary, but her heart is at rest.

OPHELIA

*P*erhaps I'm wrong; perhaps these trinkets I've accumulated over the years have nothing to do with Annie's future. The voice in my dream didn't say a blessed word about this stuff. It only said her destiny was in my hands.

I should've left it at that instead of taking it on myself to decide she needed to know everything about the treasures. Finding happy memories is all well and good, but once you start poking around in another person's life and opening up secrets they might want to keep hidden you're staring trouble in the eye.

First it was the watch. When she told me about how she'd seen and felt the fire, I thought maybe she'd just had a bad dream. I've had plenty of those. Why, there have been times I'd wake up with my heart pounding like a kettledrum because I was so scared.

This thing with the locket is different. She wasn't asleep when it happened. She felt the blow and knew where it came from. Annie didn't say how scared she was, but I could see it in her face. When I was sitting there listening to that story I was just as scared as she was, but I'm older and I've learned to keep a straight face instead of letting folks see what's picking at my insides.

After hanging on to that watch and the locket for all these years, you might think I'd be sad to see them go but I'm not. Not one iota. I say good riddance to both of them. Nothing in this world is as precious as that girl, and I'm not willing to take chances with her life.

Starting tomorrow I'm going to stop this nonsense about hunting *down memories. I'm gonna tell her it's time to go out into the world and get a job. She needs to meet people her own age and have fun. Once that happens, if she's got leftover time to spend with me I'll thank the good Lord and be happy about it.*

Soon enough I'll be dancing all over heaven with my Edward, and it'll be as sweet as it always was.

See, that's what I want for Annie. A man who'll love her the way Edward loved me. She's got a good heart and deserves to find some happiness for herself, not spend her days caring for an old lady.

THE TIME HAS COME

Weary from her late-night excursion, Ophelia does not open her eyes until after nine the next morning. Still groggy, she is slow in dressing but before she starts down the stairs she knows exactly what she will do.

Annie sits at the table with a large mug of tea and a notepad where she is scribbling her thoughts. After weeks of working with Ophelia in the apothecary, she has gleaned a thin layer of knowledge about the herbs and mixes so today she has added a scoop of coriander to the tea.

When she mentions this a puzzled look settles on Ophelia's face and she asks, "Whatever for?"

"Protection," Annie answers. "I think maybe one bad thing happened to Delia, but behind it there might be a lot of other good things, things tied to my destiny. I'd like to start wearing the locket again and see—"

"No," Ophelia answers emphatically. "That's definitely not the case." Before Annie can jump in with a differing opinion, Ophelia continues. "I had another dream last night, and this one was a lot clearer than the first."

Annie gives an eager smile, pushes the notepad aside and listens.

"I saw that same bright sun," Ophelia says, "and heard the same voice." She leans in and looks straight into Annie's eyes with no indication of a lie. "It told me that my treasures have nothing to do with your future; it said what you need to do is go into Langley, get a job and meet young people your own age."

A look of disappointment tugs at Annie's face. "That's it?"

Ophelia nods. With a look as innocent as that of a newborn babe, she adds, "The voice was explicit this time. It said there's no future in those things, only bits and pieces of meaningless old memories."

"I don't get it," Annie says. "If those things aren't tied to my future, then why am I seeing and feeling these things?"

This question Ophelia is not prepared for. She shrugs and gives the only answer that comes to mind. "It must be this house. It was here at the house that I started finding memories, so I can only guess the same thing is happening to you."

Annie has no answer. For several minutes she sits there thinking, then says, "That can't be it. The thing with the locket didn't happen here, it happened when I was back in Philadelphia."

"Maybe so," Ophelia argues, "but you brought the locket from the house."

Such a thought saddens Annie. Sifting through the things in search of a memory is like a treasure hunt; each new find brings a thrill and a burst of excitement. Now, because of a single dream, Ophelia is suggesting she give it up. Although she found it easy enough to believe in a dream that promised her destiny was to be found through one of the treasures, she now finds it hard to believe in this one. It is reminiscent of the horoscopes she used to read in the *Philadelphia Inquirer*. She chose to believe the ones that predicted a good day for romance or a day when she would find new friends, prosperity or good luck, but when it warned of trouble she laughed at the silliness of such an idea.

Finding a job now seems so ordinary, and Annie cannot stand the thought of again crunching numbers to measure how long a person will live. With sadness making her eyes appear more grey than violet, she looks at Ophelia and says, "Couldn't I just work in the apothecary? Or maybe plant a bigger garden and sell the produce?"

Although the sorrow in Annie's words weighs heavily on her heart, Ophelia forces a carefree chuckle. "This isn't Langley. The dream said you have to go into Langley and find a job."

"But that's a forty-minute drive from here. What if you need something—"

"Need something?" Ophelia cuts in. "Why, I've gotten along all these years with doing for myself. I imagine I can get along during the day when you're off at work."

Annie smiles. "So I just have to work in Langley and can still live here?"

"Of course," Ophelia replies. "I wouldn't have it any other way."

She then tells Annie that Theodore McLeary, manager of the Langley Savings and Loan, is an old and trusted friend and might be willing to help Annie find work.

"I'll call him today," she says.

Theodore McLeary owes Ophelia a favor—a big favor. Were it not for Ophelia, Maryellen would have died years earlier. That winter half the people in Langley came down with the flu. Nine people died, and Winston Barnes, the town's only doctor, was laid up with a sky-high fever. Once that happened, there was no one to take his place.

Theodore was on the verge of desperation when he called and asked if Ophelia had a remedy. That same afternoon she drove over, and for three straight days she spent every minute watching over Maryellen. On the morning of the fourth day the fever finally broke. It was then that Theodore said if Ophelia ever needed anything—anything at all—he'd be there for her.

Now she is ready to collect on that promise.

While Annie cleans up in the apothecary, Ophelia makes the call.

"The girl needs a job," she says. She does not tell Theodore anything of what has transpired, only that Annie is as dear to her as Maryellen is to him. She also doesn't mention the promise he made all those years ago.

She doesn't have to; he remembers.

"I've got a spot in the bookkeeping department," he suggests, "and it's good as hers."

The next morning when Annie leaves the house she is wearing a navy blue suit and high heels. As she pulls out of the driveway, Ophelia stands at the window watching. A tear hovers on the rim of her left eye as she prays that she has done the right thing.

MEETING MISTER MCLEARY

Annie is outside the Langley Savings and Loan at 9:35. She allowed more than twice the time necessary for the drive and has arrived almost an hour before her scheduled appointment.

She walks to the corner, looks into the window of a bakery, then turns and walks back again. Arriving too early makes her seem desperate, she reasons, so again she walks to the corner and back. This time she does not stop at the bakery. She checks her watch. Only five minutes have passed.

Crossing the street Annie walks in the other direction. The Langley Public Library is two blocks down, and before she realizes it she is standing inside.

It is like Memory House, magical in its own way. It has none of the noise of a busy office, no hum of conversation floating through the air, no clip clop of high heels trotting along hallways. There is only the soft whisper of words and a librarian who walks with silent steps. The librarian is a young woman with blonde hair and glasses perched halfway down her nose. Pretty. Not at all like Missus Culver, the school librarian Annie remembers.

Moving to the reading area, Annie lowers herself into a large leather chair. It is the color of luggage and soft as a glove. From here she can see a good part of the room. It is a room where she feels comfortable. She can smell the paper of the books and aging leather of their bindings. She lifts *The Richmond Courier* from the table and pretends to read.

A small boy comes to the desk with a single book. The librarian pulls a card from the book, stamps it and then hands it back to the lad. As she does so she says something; he nods and smiles. After him there is an elderly woman with a stack of four, maybe five books. She and the librarian have an intimate conversation; both women laugh, but Annie is too far away to hear why.

She moves to another chair, one that is at the end of the mahogany bookshelves and a bit closer to the desk. A teenager approaches and appears to ask a question. The librarian points toward the far end of the room and says something, but Annie still cannot hear what is being said. She knows only that the answer generates a smile.

As she watches people come and go, Annie starts to like the young librarian. She stands, thinking to introduce herself, straightens her skirt and starts toward the desk.

Only then does she remember to look at her watch. It is 10:28, a scant two minutes before her appointment. Darting out the door Annie breaks into long strides that are only slightly less than a run. When she walks into the bank her cheeks are flushed and her words breathy.

Theodore McLeary is exactly as Annie expected: gentlemanly, soft-spoken and silver haired. When she is ushered into his office, he stands and comes around to the front of the desk to greet her.

Once they are settled, she hands him a copy of her resume. It is the same one she used to get the job at Quality Life seven years ago. The last job listed on the resume is a small accounting firm.

He takes the paper she offers and starts to read it. "Accounting experience," he says, "that's good." When he gets to the end he flips the paper over looking for a continuation. There is none.

"Your last job was seven years ago?"

The question is casual, and he acts as though this is nothing unusual.

"No," Annie answers. "I didn't realize I'd be looking for a job so soon and haven't yet updated my resume."

"No problem," he answers. Leaning back in his chair he says, "Just fill me in on your last job."

Annie tells him about Quality Life. "I started as an underwriting assistant, and worked my way up to actuarial."

As she continues explaining various details of the job, McLeary gives an occasional nod. The expression on his face says he is pleased with what he is hearing.

After he has heard all he needs to know, Theodore McLeary offers Annie the job. "You'd be assisting Mister Bainbridge in the bookkeeping department. I think it's something you'll enjoy."

Although there has not yet been one word of discussion regarding the salary, the disappointment on her face is obvious.

McLeary sees this and adds, "I wouldn't expect you to take an assistant's salary; we'd make it commensurate with your experience."

Annie's expression doesn't change.

"You're not happy with this offer, are you?"

Annie winces and gives her head a reluctant shake.

Assuming it is the thought of being demoted to the position of an assistant, McLeary says, "Bainbridge will be retiring in less than a year, and if things work out you'll head up the department."

"It's not that," Annie says. "I was just kind of hoping to get a job where I can work with people. Ophelia said—"

"What kind of a job did you have in mind?"

Annie shrugs. "I'm not sure. Teller, maybe? Service assistant?"

"Hmmm." McLeary tents his hands in front of his face and leans into them. For a moment he is silent, thinking what to do.

"We don't have any of those openings right now," he finally says, "and I don't know how long it will be until we do have something."

"I understand," Annie replies.

When he asks if she would be willing to take the bookkeeping job until a teller position opens up, Annie says she'd rather not.

"Think it over," McLeary offers. "If you change your mind, get back to me."

Annie thanks him then leaves the bank. On the way out she is smiling.

By the time she reaches the sidewalk, Annie knows exactly what she is going to do. She crosses the street and heads back to the library.

Once inside she does not go directly to the desk; instead she walks through the stacks, touches her fingers to the books, occasionally straightening one or turning it right side up, sniffing the smell of leather bindings and imagining the decades of people who have come and gone through these very same aisles.

A feeling of familiarity settles over Annie, a feeling much the same as she felt that first night at Memory House. She has had one thought in mind ever since she left the bank, but it is not until her hand lifts a book titled *Here is Where I Belong* that she knows for certain.

This is where she belongs.

⊙══◆══⊙

It is late afternoon when Annie arrives back at Memory House. As she passes through the hall she catches the aroma of the library. For the moment the fragrance of ink on paper is her favorite, and the potpourri reminds her of it.

Ophelia is in the kitchen. Annie comes in and hugs her from behind.

"I got a job," Annie says. Her words have the sound of happiness woven through them. "It's part time, three days a week."

Ophelia turns. "Three days a week? Is that all Theodore had to offer?"

"The job isn't at the bank, it's at the library."

"The library?"

Annie nods. "Mister McLeary offered me a job at the bank, but it was as an assistant in the bookkeeping department." She hesitates a moment then wrinkles her nose. "You don't find happiness working with numbers. I know that only too well."

Annie tells of her experience at the library. She describes in detail the feel of the books and the faces of those coming and going. When she has finished she gives a wistful sigh.

"Numbers are only numbers," she says, "but books and stories, that's where the magic is."

Ophelia thinks back on the stories Edward once told and doesn't disagree.

ANNIE

*I*f a year ago you'd told me I would be working as an assistant librarian, I'd have laughed in your face. Not me, I would have said, I'm an actuarial.

Back then I thought numbers were the measurement of life. The things that counted were the date you were born, the number of years you're supposed to live, the amount of money you earn, the cost of your car, the number of rooms in your house—anything and everything could be boiled down to a number. Instead of using a person's name, I added up all those other numbers and filed them under a Social Security Number.

Even my relationship with Michael had a number. We did one of those magazine tests to see if we were each other's perfect match and scored 100. Perfectly matched, according to the article. When we'd argue and be totally at odds with one another, I'd pull the copy of that test from my nightstand drawer, read it again and convince myself that everything would work out fine—not based on what my heart was telling me, but just on the numbers. How foolish is that?

I should have realized there is no number for happiness. You can't hold it in your hand, touch it or measure it; you just know it's there. And having it makes a gigantic difference in your life. It's a shame it took me so long to figure that out.

I'm excited about working at the library. Just being there gives me a good feeling. It's as if I know something good is going to happen but have no idea what it is.

When Ophelia first told me about feeling the memories other people had left behind I thought she was just an eccentric old lady, but I've come to see she's way smarter than I am.

The world is full of things that can't be numbered or even explained; I know that sounds like a lot of hocus-pocus, but it's not. Before you find the magic of life you have to open yourself up to the possibility of it being there. When I was walking around the library I could practically see the years of people who had passed through those very same aisles. I imagined ladies in long skirts and men in striped vests searching for just the right book. I could feel the magic of that place, and I wanted to be part of it.

The truth is I would have worked there for free if I had to. Luckily Giselle offered me a job.

THE LIBRARY

For five days Annie thinks of nothing but the library. Twice she drives into Langley just to visit it again. On the second trip she brings Ophelia, and they stroll arm in arm through the stacks.

Whispering as if it were a cardinal sin to speak loudly, she asks, "Do you feel the magic of this place?"

Ophelia nods, but she knows Annie feels something that she does not.

As they walk Annie touches her fingers lovingly to the spine of first one book and then another, and Ophelia wonders if the girl's power to find memories is growing stronger as her own grows weaker. It has been years since a relic of the past has called to her and given up a special memory.

Such a thought sits uncomfortably on Ophelia's shoulders. Not because she is saddened by the loss of her own power, but because she fears Annie may unleash some unknown terror. Through the years this finding of memories has been simply a pleasant distraction for Ophelia, but with Annie it's something more.

Annie pulls a T.S. Lawrence book from the shelf and thumbs through the pages.

"I think there's a secret hidden here," she whispers. "A secret I'm supposed to find."

The book is old, the spine crackled and bent back on the bottom edge. The gilt title is dulled and almost unreadable, but when Annie sets the book back on the shelf Ophelia sees it is *Seven Pillars of Wisdom*.

"Why did you pick that book?" Ophelia asks.

Annie shrugs. "I don't know. My hand just went to it."

On the first Monday of October Annie starts her new job. Instead of dressing in the conservative blue suit, she wears beige gabardine slacks and a sweater the violet of her eyes. There is no way of knowing whether it is the excitement of this day or simply the warmth of the sweater, but when she kisses Ophelia goodbye her face is flushed with color.

Before Giselle arrives to unlock the door, Annie is waiting on the steps.

"I guess you're anxious to get started," Giselle says with a laugh.

Annie answers that she is indeed and follows Giselle through the door.

Although she has spent three afternoons walking through the stacks, there is still much to be learned. Most of the first day is spent studying the Dewey decimal system and familiarizing herself with the library layout.

On the second day, Giselle produces a metal cart loaded with books and assigns Annie the task of replacing each book in the proper spot. Although the cart is piled high and heavy to push, Annie smiles. She handles each book with the same reverence Ophelia uses with her treasures.

Her day is supposed to end at five o'clock, but Annie stays until Giselle locks the door at seven. Once the metal cart is cleared she logs in the books returned during the busy afternoon and stacks them on the empty cart.

Tuesday is Annie's day off, but she tells Giselle she would be happy to come in to re-shelve the new stack of books.

Giselle laughs and says such a thing is not necessary.

"You don't have to pay me," Annie adds. "I'll do it as a volunteer."

"You worked hard today," Giselle replies. "Take the day off so you'll be ready for Wednesday."

Annie hears a hidden promise. "Why? What will I be doing?"

Giselle smiles. "I'm going to let you start working the desk."

Even though she knows she will miss being away from the library for a full day, Annie is cheered by thoughts of thunking down the date stamp and chatting with the people who come through with an armful of books.

On the drive home she can already picture herself sitting behind the desk.

It is early October, but the leaves have begun to turn and a chill has settled in the air. The garden is ready for winter. Most of the flowers and herbs have been clipped and are now on the drying racks in the apothecary. There are few chores left to do—a bit of dusting perhaps and a quick run through with the vacuum cleaner. Still Annie rises early on Tuesday morning.

She has breakfast on the table when Ophelia comes down.

"I'm sorry about the tea," Annie says. "I put an extra scoop in, but it's still rather weak." She sets a mug on the table and fills it. Instead of the rich golden color Ophelia is used to, the tea is a pale shadow of its former self.

"If you want I can make another pot," Annie adds.

Ophelia takes a sip and says, "This tea tastes fine." She knows the dandelion tea is weak because she has mixed it with a large amount of chamomile. After ridding herself of the watch and the locket, Ophelia still fears Annie might discover dangerous memories in the other treasures. She is praying a milder tea will lessen the girl's ability to connect with such things.

As Annie carries a basket of blueberry muffins to the table she tells of her intent to ride Ethan Allen's bicycle again today.

"I feel that I'm getting to know the boy," she says, "and I like him."

The expression on Ophelia's face droops. "Oh," she says. It is only a single syllable, but it slides downhill like a runaway wagon.

"What's wrong?" Annie asks.

"I rather hoped we could go shopping today," Ophelia replies. Because it is the first thing that comes to mind she adds, "I need some new dish towels."

"No problem," Annie says. "I'll ride the bicycle later."

The thought of the bicycle prompts Annie to tell of the things she has heard. "Ethan Allen used this bicycle to run errands."

She now calls the boy by name, not just once in a while but every time. "People paid him for doing it. I've heard the jingle of change in his pocket."

"That could have been anything," Ophelia replies. "Kids playing Tiddlywinks in their backyard, maybe."

"It wasn't," Annie says. There is no doubt in her voice.

Annie still has Ethan Allen's ball, and every night she sleeps with it beneath her pillow. Sometimes she dreams of the boy but has never seen his face.

She has seen a dime dropping into his small hand and felt the racing of his heart. It has the thump-thump-thump of a frightened rabbit, but she has yet to discover why.

NOVEMBER

It is a month to the day since Annie started working at the library. She now does everything Giselle does. She has a key to the front entrance, and on Monday morning she unlocks the door. Monday is Giselle's day off.

It is on this first Monday of November that Annie finds what she has been looking for.

The day starts off as a rather ordinary one. Annie sips her coffee, logs in the returned books and adds them to the stack Giselle has left on the metal cart. The books will be shelved at the end of the day, when and if she has time.

It is not yet nine-thirty when a young man comes to the desk asking for assistance.

"I'm looking for a Civil War reference book," he says. "Something with in-depth detail on the battle of Shiloh."

Now familiar with the historical reference section, Annie leads him to the spot. There are nine shelves of books on the Civil War. He eyes the section then turns to Annie.

"Any idea which one deals specifically with Shiloh?"

"Not really," she answers, "but I'll check the index file."

For most of the morning Annie is back and forth with the young man. She gives him suggestions on first one book and then another, and when the very one he needs is missing she spends an hour searching for it.

In between trips back and forth to the historical reference section, she signs books in and out, answers a call and smiles at the patrons who come her way.

This day is busier than usual, but Annie doesn't mind. At lunchtime she remains at the desk and nibbles a tuna fish sandwich brought from home. The stack on the metal cart grows larger as more books are returned, but there is no time for shelving them. That's a task to be done in the off times. It is not one that takes precedence over other things.

At seven o'clock, when the last of the library patrons have left the building, Annie locks the door. The stack of books on the return cart is now considerably larger, and it has been a long day.

For a moment she considers leaving the books for Giselle to replace on Tuesday. That has been their arrangement thus far, and Giselle has never complained about it. But Giselle is expecting a baby in two months, and Annie has seen how her steps have grown heavier. When she squats to replace a book on the bottom shelf there is a laborious grunt, and it's the same when she stretches to reach one of the higher shelves.

After a quick call to Ophelia to say she will be an hour or so late coming home, Annie wheels the cart from behind the desk and heads for the fiction area.

Novels are stacked on the top shelf of the cart, reference and textbooks on the lower shelf.

Annie has learned to look first at the index number on the spine. In a single glance it tells her where the book belongs. Were she to stop and read the author's name and title, the job would take twice, maybe three times as long.

Novels are alphabetized according to the author's last name. Annie starts in the As, replacing a worn copy of Louisa May Alcott's *Little Women* and moves along until she slips Thornton Wilder's *Our Town* back onto the shelf. In less than twenty minutes the top shelf of the cart is empty.

She moves to the reference department. These books take longer because they are arranged first by subject matter, then by author name. All too often it means running from one stack to another that is located four or five aisles away.

Annie is down to the last four books when she reaches for a heavy book marked for the Legal section. The moment her hand touches it, she knows. A shiver runs from the tip of her fingers to her heart, then splinters and scatters itself throughout her body. Even before Annie looks at the title of this book, she is certain she has found what she has been looking for.

She lifts the book and holds it with both hands. It is an oversized volume with a burgundy leather binding and gold leaf letters that read *The Wisdom of Judicial Judgment in the Practice of Law.* At the bottom is the name of the author: Ethan Allen Doyle.

This is her bicycle boy. He has grown to be a man, a man of law and principles. A man who has authored a book.

Leaving the last three books on the cart, Annie wheels it back to the desk and goes to the library's computer. Entering the name Ethan Allen Doyle, she begins with the Virginia judicial records.

At first she finds nothing but continues to scroll through what is a seemingly endless list of judges. There are individual listings for each court—Bankruptcy Court, Civil Court, Criminal Court, Divorce and Property settlement.

None have an Ethan Allen Doyle registered.

It is over an hour before she happens on the listing of United States Court Officers for the Eastern District of Virginia. Two pages down she hits the listing for Family Court Judge Ethan Allen Doyle.

"Yes!" she shouts and bounds out of the chair.

According to the listing Judge Ethan Allen Doyle sits on the bench of Family Court in Wyattsville, Virginia, a town less than an hour's drive from Burnsville.

Annie's first thought is to call Ophelia and give her the good news, but she wants to do more; she wants to be there so she can see the amazement on Ophelia's face. Finding the book proves her destiny is with the bicycle boy himself. There is no other explanation.

Now in a rush to lock up the library and get home, she hurriedly shuts down the computer, gathers her things, tucks the book under her arm and heads for the door.

Had she scrolled down another few lines she might have noticed the listing for Judge Doyle was dated June 1994.

Before she leaves Langley, Annie stops at the liquor store and buys a bottle of champagne. In her mind finding the bicycle boy is definitely cause for celebration.

When Annie arrives back at the house she hurries to the kitchen where she is certain she will find Ophelia. The small lamp on the table is lit, but the overhead is off and the stove is cold. There is a note on the table.

In a handwritten scrawl, Ophelia says she is tired and going to bed early. "Nothing to worry about," she adds.

Next to the note is a covered plate of sliced chicken and pear salad.

Dumbfounded, Annie stands looking at the note. It is a letdown in what was to have been a moment of victory. She tries to convince herself that the celebration will be just as sweet tomorrow morning, but the argument is unconvincing.

Setting the bottle of champagne in the refrigerator she turns, circles back through the hallway and tiptoes up the staircase. She wants to believe there is a possibility Ophelia is not yet asleep, in which case it would be okay to gently tap on the door and ask if she'd like to hear the news.

Standing outside the door Annie hears nothing. No rustling around, no whispering sounds of radio music. She waits several minutes then eases the door open. Ophelia is turned on her side, sound asleep.

Annie closes the door and retreats down the stairs.

She is bursting with the excitement of having found the bicycle boy and has no one to tell. The thrill of her discovery is somehow lessened.

For a long while Annie sits at the table alone. She thumbs through the book, reading an odd sentence here and there, but it is hard to concentrate on the words. When she tires of reading, she begins to imagine Ethan Allen's expression when he learns his bicycle is now good as new and she's been riding it around the streets of Burnsville for over three months.

This image settles in Annie's head, and she starts to smile.

Since Ophelia is not available to hear the news, Annie considers calling Ethan Allen himself. She pulls out her cell phone, clicks Safari and searches the White Pages directory for Wyattsville, Virginia.

Three Doyles are found. None of them are listed as Ethan Allen, yet she copies the address and phone number for all three.

It is after ten when she dials the first number—a listing for Barbara Jean Doyle.

As Annie listens to the phone ring she nervously twists the pen in her fingers. On the third ring, she takes to drawing tiny little circles along the side of the paper. Shortly after the eighth ring someone picks up the receiver.

"George, is that you?" a woman shouts. "It better not be you 'cause I warned you about calling me at this hour!"

Annie has practiced what she will say, but now the words are stuck in her throat. Before she pulls her thoughts together, the woman grumbles, "Damn nutbugger!" and slams down the receiver.

Rather than risk the ire of someone related to Ethan Allen, Annie sets the paper aside.

The phone calls will have to wait until tomorrow; tonight the only thing she can do is place the Spalding ball under her pillow and hope for a dream to come.

TUESDAY

For the first time since she began work at the library Annie is glad to have the day off. She has her day planned. Shortly after nine she will call all three numbers, locate Ethan Allen Doyle, then drive over to Wyattsville and meet him.

Although it has been a sleepless night Annie is up early. When she hears Ophelia's footsteps on the stair she scurries through the hall and waits at the bottom landing.

"I've got the most wonderful news!" she says.

Feeling the weight of her years, Ophelia is still trying to shrug off the after effects of the two sleeping pills she took last night. She rubs her hand across her right eye and says, "News? What news?" There is no excitement in her voice; her words are as flat and thin as a sheet of paper.

"I've found Ethan Allen!" When Ophelia's expression remains the same Annie adds, "The bicycle boy!"

This is like a splash of cold water on Ophelia's face. She is now fully awake. "Found him where?"

"He's a judge; lives in Wyattsville." As they walk to the kitchen Annie rattles on about finding the book, searching the name and then finding the addresses and phone numbers for all three Doyles.

Ophelia is not smiling. In fact, the expression on her face is one of apprehension—or perhaps fear. When she hears Annie plans to go meet this man, she speaks up. In a short burst of words she says, "Don't do it!"

"Don't do what?" Annie replies.

"Don't go in search of this man," Ophelia says. Even though there has not been time enough for the thought to settle in her head, she adds, "I've got a bad feeling about it."

This shocks Annie. "How can you possibly…" She lifts the hook off the table and shows Ophelia. "He's a lawyer, a judge even! A man like that isn't one to—"

"Doesn't matter," Ophelia says. "There's a bad memory attached to that bicycle; I can feel it in my bones."

"There are good memories too," Annie argues. "I've felt them."

This is the first time they are at odds with one another, and both women are adamant in their opinions. When Annie sets breakfast on the table, Ophelia barely touches the food and a heavy silence settles over them. There is only the clatter of a spoon as Annie stirs honey into her tea and the sorrowful sound of Ophelia's labored breath.

It is Annie who finally speaks. "Let's work this out. We'll drive over together. You can meet Judge Doyle and if you still feel the same after meeting him, we'll give him back the bicycle, come home and I'll not mention it again."

Ophelia would prefer Annie get rid of the bicycle right now and never mention the boy's name again, but she knows this will not happen.

"If I agree," she says, "then you'll give up thoughts of chasing after *any* of the treasures?" There is considerable emphasis on the word "any". Ophelia wants to be rid of this worry. For too many years she has lived in the shadow of other people's memories. She wants something more for Annie.

Although Annie is reluctant to give such an all-encompassing promise, she nods. The truth is that none of the other treasures have spoken to her. Not the snow globe, not the quilt, not the doll and not even the Lannigan family Bible.

Once Annie gives her nod of agreement, Ophelia picks up a spoon and begins to eat the honeyed oatmeal.

As soon as the breakfast dishes have been cleared away, Annie dials the first number on her list. It is Barbara Jean Doyle, the woman from last night. Annie hopes this is a sister or cousin perhaps, not a wife.

Before the second ring, the same woman answers the phone. This time her voice is pleasant enough, but when Annie asks for Ethan Allen Doyle she claims no one by that name lives there.

"Do you know him?" Annie asks. "Or can you maybe suggest someone else who might know him?"

"Afraid not," the woman says. "Doyle is a pretty common name; there's likely dozens of them right here in Wyattsville."

"No," Annie says. "Just three."

The second call is to a J. Fred Doyle, and it is no more productive than the first. When he says he's never heard of an Ethan Allen Doyle, Annie adds that he's a judge.

"Have you ever heard of a Judge Doyle?" she asks.

"Certainly not!" Fred answers. "I'm a law-abiding citizen, and if you're trying to suggest anything else—"

"I'm not," Annie assures him, but before she can rephrase the question she hears the click of the receiver.

The third and last name on the list is Oliver Doyle.

Annie dials the number and waits. After listening to a countless number of rings she hangs up. There is no answer and no answering machine.

The remainder of the day is spent reading passages from the book and redialing Oliver Doyle's number

Five times she tries, but each time there is only the ring of the phone. No answer.

It is nearing suppertime when Annie decides there has to be something wrong with the line.

"Even if he isn't at home," she tells Ophelia, "there'd be an answering machine."

Ophelia of course does not agree with such logic.

"That has to be it," Annie reasons. "I'll have to drive over to Wyattsville and check it out."

Before Annie has closed her mouth, Ophelia has pulled her coat from the closet and is ready to leave. Come what may, she will be glad to put an end to Annie's investigation of the treasures.

In Wyattsville

The address for O. E. Doyle is a townhouse on Chestnut Street. The front windows are dark, but in the back of the building there is a light so it would seem someone is at home. Annie suggests Ophelia wait in the car while she goes to check.

"If it's Judge Doyle, I'll come back for you," she says.

"Make certain you do," Ophelia warns.

Although she has agreed to wait in the car, Ophelia keeps a sharp eye on the door of the building. If Annie steps one foot across the threshold, she is ready to go after her.

The building has no front porch, just a small stoop with no outside light. Ophelia can see Annie because of the white sweater she is wearing, but everything else is lost in the darkness. After a minute the door opens, and a yellow light floods the stoop.

Ophelia sees a man standing in the doorway. The light is behind him, so it's impossible to see his face.

Although it is what she has been wishing for, Annie is unprepared for the reality of him standing there. She struggles to find the right words. She planned to give a lighthearted laugh and say, "Hey, Ethan Allen, I've come to return your bicycle." But instead she says, "Judge Doyle?"

The words are too formal and too ordinary, but once they are spoken she cannot take them back.

The man in the doorway nods. "Yes. What can I do for you?"

He is handsomer and considerably younger than Annie imagined. "I have your bicycle."

"My bicycle?"

Annie nods. She turns and points a finger toward Ophelia who is sitting in the car at the end of the driveway. "My friend is actually the one who found it, but back then it was covered in rust and—"

"I'm not certain I understand..."

When Ophelia sees Annie wave a finger toward the car she assumes this is a signal that the bicycle boy has been found. She climbs from the car and starts toward the house.

Annie again motions toward the driveway. "I have the bike in the trunk of my car. Ophelia found it at the Sisters of Mercy Thrift Shop, and she kept it because of the memories..."

Seeing Annie point to the car a second time pushes Ophelia's worry button.

"Dear God," she mumbles, "please don't let anything happen to this child."

Ophelia starts moving faster and then breaks into a wobbly run. A few feet from the stoop her knee gives out, and she starts to fall. There is a whoosh of air as she grapples for balance and seconds later a loud thud.

Annie turns in time to see her hit the ground. "Ophelia!"

When she runs to help, the man in the doorway follows. As he lifts Ophelia to her feet he asks, "Are you alright?"

It is only then that Ophelia gets a look at his face. She gasps.

"Edward?" When he nods, she collapses into a dead faint.

"We'd better get her inside," he suggests. "I'll call for a doctor."

Together they carry Ophelia inside and place her on the sofa. He disappears into the kitchen and returns with a cold cloth. "This might help," he says and hands the cloth to Annie.

The next several minutes are spent trying to revive Ophelia. There is no discussion about the bicycle or anything else,

Once she opens her eyes and sits up the conversation resumes. Now that Ophelia is calm and the man's face is clearly visible, she can see he is not her Edward. There is only a slight resemblance. He has the same light hair and eyes but is taller, broader in the shoulder and doesn't have the cleft chin of Edward.

"I'm sorry to cause such a fuss," she says. "For a moment I thought you were my Edward."

He smiles. "You're partially right. Edward is my middle name."

It is now Annie's turn to look confused. "But I asked if you were—"

"You asked if I was Judge Doyle," he cuts in. "And I am. Judge Oliver Edward Doyle. But as far as a bicycle is concerned…"

Annie closes her eyes and shakes her head. "You're not the right one. I'm trying to find Ethan Allen Doyle. He's a family court judge here in Wyattsville."

Before Annie can say anything more, Oliver begins to laugh. It is a warm rich sound that fills the room. "You're a little late. Ethan Allen is my dad. He retired from the bench six years ago."

The disappointment on Annie's face is obvious.

Oliver sees this and says, "I'm sorry."

"It's not your fault," Annie says. "It's just…" She tells the story of how Ophelia found the bicycle that belonged to Ethan Allen Doyle, and she had now restored it.

"How did you find out that particular bicycle belonged to my dad?" Oliver asks.

Ophelia speaks before Annie has the chance to do so. "It's a long story," she says, "too long for tonight." She smiles at Annie, and there is an unspoken understanding that the finding of memories will remain their secret.

"Okay." Oliver laughs. "So let's say you knew the bicycle belonged to Dad. How did you know to look for him here in Wyattsville?"

When Annie tells of finding the book that Ethan Allen authored, there is a tear in her eye.

"I have that same book," Oliver says. He crosses to the bookshelf and pulls out a copy of *The Wisdom of Judicial Judgment in the Practice of Law*. He hands it to Annie. "Dad gave this to me the day I passed the bar. Look at the inscription."

Annie opens the book and reads: "Judge fairly and wisely. Remember, but for the grace of God and the kindness of others, it could have been me standing on the other side of the bench."

They talk for a long while and before the evening ends Oliver suggests Annie keep the bicycle.

"I already have an English racer," he says.

As he walks the ladies to the car he gives Annie a shy smile and says, "I'm a lot like my dad."

Annie turns to him. "In what way?"

Oliver shrugs. "Well, I'm a judge and I like bicycling." He hesitates a moment then adds, "Maybe we could ride together one afternoon."

Annie is not certain whether this is an invitation or simply a passing comment. She smiles and says, "I doubt I could keep up with an English racer."

"Oh, I'm sure you can," Oliver says. He leans down and whispers in her ear, "When I want to, I can pedal pretty darn slow."

AND SO IT HAPPENS...

The next day Oliver stops by the library. He tells Annie he happened to be in the neighborhood, but actually he's driven thirty miles out of his way.

"I wanted to make certain your friend is okay," he says.

While this is partly true, it also gives him a reason for being there.

"She's fine." Annie smiles. "It's nice of you to be concerned."

Although she can't explain why, Annie is glad to see Oliver again. When he invites her to lunch she says yes.

He suggests the Italian restaurant at the far end of Grove Street. It is a fifteen-minute walk, and as they cross Butler Boulevard he loops his arm through hers.

Annie has planned to take her usual one-hour lunch break, but once they start talking time slips away. She has a million questions about Ethan Allen's boyhood, but Oliver has few answers. He knows only that a grandma named Olivia raised his dad and that he adored her.

"Something happened to Dad's parents," Oliver says, "but he never really talks about it."

In time the conversation segues into other topics. Oliver talks about his growing up years, and Annie tells how she came to Memory House. She doesn't mention Ophelia's gift for finding memories, and when the subject of how she knew the bicycle was Ethan Allen's comes up she turns it off with a laugh.

"I believe one of the Sisters at the thrift shop told Ophelia," she says. It is not the truth, but it's more believable so she leaves it at that.

It is almost three o'clock when Annie returns to the library.

"I'm so sorry," she tells Giselle. "I can't imagine how I lost track of time."

"I can." Giselle chuckles. "Your young man is rather handsome and quite charming."

"Oh, he's not my boyfriend," Annie replies, but while the words still hang in the air she already sees Oliver in a new light.

On Friday the library telephone rings and Giselle answers. She walks back to the stacks where Annie is shelving some books.

"You have a phone call." She winks and gives a knowing smile. "It sounds like that handsome young man you claim isn't your boyfriend."

Annie hurries to the phone and finds it is Oliver Doyle.

They talk for a few moments. He tells her he enjoyed their lunch and was wondering if she'd like to go bicycle riding on Saturday. As if in an effort to convince her, he adds, "The forecast is for good weather."

She needs no convincing. She has been hoping he'd call.

"I'd love to," she says and gives him directions to Memory House. "It's at the end of Haber Street, past the sign and the big weeping willow."

They settle on ten-thirty as a good time, and when Annie hangs up a smile curls the corners of her mouth. She cannot say exactly what it is, but something about Oliver draws her to him. It is more than knowing he is the son of her bicycle boy. It is his easy smile and the timbre of his voice.

Saturday morning dawns with a bright sun and gentle breeze. It is a perfect day for bicycling, brisk but not cold. The leaves on the oaks have already turned, and from time to time a small gust of wind sends them swirling in a cornucopia of color.

Annie dresses in jeans and a purple sweater that brings out the violet color in her eyes. She twists her hair into a clip then adds a bit of mascara and a swish of pink lip gloss. When Oliver pulls into the driveway it is barely ten-fifteen, but she is ready. She darts out the door before he has pulled his bicycle from the trunk.

"You're early," she says.

He lets his eyes linger on her face then nods and grins. "But I see you're ready for me."

She laughs with delight. It is obvious that both of them have been looking forward to this moment,

They climb onto their bicycles and start back down the long driveway. He is riding a sleek black ten-speed racer with a narrow seat and low handlebars. She is on a bicycle that is almost twice the age of Oliver. After all those months of polishing, it glistens in the morning sun. The old bicycle is heavier and slower, but Annie doesn't mind. She is used to it. Oliver sees this and paces himself accordingly. He pedals slowly and stays beside her.

Side by side they pull onto Haber Street and at the end of the street they turn onto Lakeside Drive, the road that circles the pond and comes around to rejoin Haber at the far end. Lakeside is a quiet street lined with quaint Victorian cottages and small Cape Cod houses. From time to time they can hear the squawking of the two ducks that spend the winter on the pond. Always the same two, they stay even though the others leave. The pond never freezes, and each morning Ophelia scatters biscuit crumbs along the edge of the water. They stay because this has become home to them, just as it is now home to Annie.

They ride at a leisurely pace, and she tells him of that dark night she happened upon Memory House.

"I believe that there's a providence that puts you in the place where you're supposed to be at just the moment you're supposed to be there," she says.

He smiles at her and agrees. Although he doesn't say so, he is thankful that such providence also set her on his doorstep.

It is almost one o'clock when they finally pedal back up the driveway and bring their bikes to a stop. Annie's nose has turned pink in the crisp air, but she is laughing and happy.

"Ophelia insisted that I invite you to lunch," she tells him. "She wants to thank you for your kindness. She's made a delicious stew with vegetables from the garden."

Oliver needs no convincing.

"That sounds wonderful," he says and follows her into the house. The truth is he would have stayed if Annie offered nothing more than a few more minutes of her time. Already he is thinking of their next date and well beyond that. He can imagine himself holding her in his arms and tasting the sweetness of her kiss.

Ophelia is there to greet him as soon as he steps inside the door.

"I'm glad you came," she says and takes his hand in hers. "You were so gentlemanly when I fainted on your doorstep."

Her voice is soft and her words welcoming. With his hand in hers she can sense he is a man with good memories. This thought settles comfortably in her heart. He is the sort of man she has been hoping Annie would meet.

They gather around the wicker table on the back porch. There is sun but no wind, so Oliver sheds his jacket and drapes it over the back of his chair. Ophelia sits in the chair across from him as Annie serves the stew.

"This is Ophelia's own recipe," she says proudly. "You'll never in all your life taste a better stew." She doesn't mention that this is because Ophelia adds herbs few people know of and fewer still have the skill to use.

After a single bite Oliver grins and says he is inclined to agree.

When the bowls have been emptied Annie brews a pot of hibiscus tea. They sit at the table soaking up the warmth of the day, the food and each other. Eventually the subject rolls around to Ethan Allen, and Oliver says he knows only that Grandma Olivia raised his dad.

"I'm named after her," he says. "Dad never talks about his life before he came to live with her, but he sure did love her. Every year on her birthday we visited her grave and took flowers." He gives a shy smile then adds, "It became such a tradition that I still do it."

Ophelia smiles at this thought. Now she is certain Oliver is the man she wants for Annie. Although there is still a fair amount of tea left, Ophelia scoops up the half-full teapot and makes off with it.

"I'll freshen this up," she says.

In the kitchen she sets a fresh pot of water on to boil and reaches for the special tin of dandelion tea she keeps at the back of the cupboard. When the tea is ready she carries it to the table and fills all three cups. This is a brew that enables people to see the truth. Oliver will see the beauty of Annie, if he hasn't already, and Annie will see the strength of him.

As for Ophelia, she will watch young people falling in love as she and Edward once did, and for to her nothing is sweeter than that memory.

As the Days Pass...

The bicycling date is followed by several others. An afternoon drive, dinner out, the movies, leisurely walks and on a number of occasions they sit with Ophelia in the front parlor where the fireplace is lit.

It pleases Ophelia to see them together. It is a reminder of the times she and Edward sat in this very same room. As she watches Oliver take Annie's hand, Ophelia can almost feel Edward's fingertips touching hers.

Before the month is out, Oliver is a regular at Memory House. He is there several times a week and often brings a small gift for Ophelia: a plant, a tin of cookies, a box of chocolates.

On Thanksgiving Day Ophelia roasts a huge turkey and invites people she has known for over thirty years to join them. Oliver comes and brings her a large bouquet of yellow chrysanthemums. Although she sputters, "Oh, you shouldn't have," the delight on her face is obvious.

The extension leaf is in the dining table, which now stretches to nearly the full length of the room. When they sit for dinner they are eleven, but there are twelve chairs. The empty chair sits beside Ophelia; it is for Edward.

"He has been with me every Thanksgiving since…"

She smiles and keeps the last part of the thought to herself. She knows that she alone can feel his presence. In the quiet of her mind she tells Edward he is what she is most thankful for.

You and now Annie, she thinks.

The table is overflowing with dishes the guests have brought: candied sweet potatoes, jelled cranberry sauce, corn pudding, string beans with bits of bacon and two baskets piled high with the biscuits Annie has made. On the sideboard there is an assortment of pies, cakes and cookies enough to last throughout the week. As the bowls are passed from one guest to another there is talk of food, football and the unseasonably warm weather. Once all the plates are filled the conversation dies away, and there is only the clacking of forks and an occasional comment about the food.

When Oliver says, "This turkey is the best I've ever tasted," Ophelia makes a mental note to tell Annie the secret is the purple spotted flowers of the catnip plant. Dried and ground to a powder, a small pinch has been added to the herbs rubbed into the skin of the turkey. She will also share the old wives' tale handed down to her that even the tiniest bit of such a powder increases the bond between people. Friends will remain friends, and love will last forever.

Annie and Oliver sit directly across from Ophelia, and from the edge of her eye she can see the affection that passes between them. When he asks for this or that item from the far end of the table, his hands linger on hers as she passes him the dish. He is as Edward was that first Thanksgiving.

Once everyone has eaten their fill, Ophelia sits with her guests in the front parlor as Annie and Oliver clear the table and clean the kitchen. As they work they talk of the days to come and of the things they look forward to doing together. He says in the spring a circus comes to the fairgrounds in Dorchester and tells of how in a single day the tents are set up and wagons of food appear.

"We'll definitely want to go to that," he adds.

She nods agreeably, and he notices the tiny green sparkle in her eye.

This is how it is with love. People see things that no one else notices. A stray lock of hair pulled loose by a breeze, a smile that tilts higher on one side than it does on the other, a crooked finger, a flicker of green in eyes that are a violet hue.

Once the last dishes have been put away, they return to the parlor and join the other guests. It is almost eight, and several guests have already left. The remaining few soon follow, saying the hour is late and morning comes early.

When everyone else is gone, Ophelia suggests Annie and Oliver take a blanket and sit by the pond.

"At this time of year you can see Orion," she says, "but it's only visible in the winter sky. Come spring it will be gone."

Ophelia knows there is a different magic in the winter sky, and that special magic is what she wishes for Annie. She pulls the thick comforter from the closet and hands it to Oliver. It is a thing filled with memories, memories she knows Annie will feel.

Once they are gone, Ophelia trudges up the stairs to the loft. She slips into her nightdress and climbs into bed. As she searches the sky for the string of stars, she feels Edward's breath on her cheek.

"I thought you would come tonight," she says. "I felt it this afternoon."

"Yes, I know," he whispers. "I brought you those memories of our years together."

Ophelia smiles. "You are like the stars, always there but hidden by the bright light of day."

He chuckles, and she feels the warmth of him. "Someday we will again be together, and you will grow weary of having me constantly beside you."

She hears the laugh but knows what her answer will be.

"Never," she replies. "Never."

⚬━━✦━━⚬

Bundled in sweaters and wool socks, Annie and Oliver lie side by side looking up at the stars. Her head is cradled in the crook of his arm, and when she turns to him they are only a breath apart. In his face she can see traces of the bicycle boy as she imagined him.

A thought comes to her and she asks, "Do you have photos of when you were a kid?"

He scrunches his nose as if he is thinking then replies, "Not at the house, but my mom has albums filled with them."

"I'd love to see one," she says.

He tells her his parents now live in Florida and promises to have his mom send a picture.

For a long while they talk about the events of the day, but in time the conversation fades away and they lie together silently. At midnight when the night is at its darkest and the stars their brightest, he whispers that being here is wonderful.

"Ophelia and Edward used to do this all the time," Annie says.

"I can see why," he answers.

Oliver turns on his side and lifts himself onto his elbow. For the first time he tells Annie he has fallen in love with her.

"Hopelessly and irrevocably," he says, and without further words he leans down and presses his lips to hers.

This time it is more than a kiss; this time it is a promise.

In the smallest hours of the morning as Oliver is driving back to Wyattsville, he remembers Annie's request for a boyhood photo. He knows she believes he will look as his father once did, and this triggers a thought in his mind. He has already planned a gift for her, but perhaps he could do something more. Something unforgettable.

CHRISTMAS

For two weeks Oliver has been planning his surprise but says nothing to Annie. Although they have moved on to talking about the future rather than the past, there are still times when she peppers him with questions about his father. In her mind Ethan Allen is still a boy, a lad who pockets dimes and runs errands.

"I think he was afraid of somebody," she says. "Do you recall him talking about anything like that?"

Oliver laughs. "Dad, afraid? Never."

When Annie suggests it is something worth asking about, Oliver shakes his head.

"That was almost seventy years ago. I doubt he even remembers."

"He'd remember the bicycle," Annie says confidently. "I know he would."

Such discussions inevitably lead to tales of Oliver's boyhood, but there is little he can tell of his father's. It is just such a conversation that prompts him to plan the surprise.

Oliver's first call is to his father in Florida.

"I was wondering if you and Mom could come up for Christmas," he asks.

"Wouldn't it be better for you to come down?" Ethan Allen replies. "The weather's great and—"

Oliver cuts in. "There's somebody special I want you to meet."

"Ah ha!" Ethan Allen laughs. "It's about time. I was beginning to worry you'd end up a bachelor."

There is so much Oliver could say about Annie, but he says nothing other than she is somebody special. Ophelia he doesn't mention at all. The surprise he is planning is for all of them...and perhaps for himself also.

Annie's curiosity has piqued his; now Oliver also wants to hear the story.

⌘

Christmas morning dawns bright and cold. During the night a dusting of snow has fallen, and the trees are frosted with sprinkles of ice.

At breakfast Ophelia and Annie exchange gifts. Ophelia pulls a small box from her pocket and hands it to Annie.

"My mama gave this to me the day I got married," she says. "Now I'd like you to have it."

When Annie opens the box the gift is a cameo brooch. It is circled with a rim of gold.

"Oh," she says, "it's beautiful!" Although she is still dressed in her bathrobe she pins the cameo to her lapel.

For Ophelia Annie has gotten a new robe. One that is the blue of the sky with pockets deep enough for the treasures Ophelia often carries about.

After the exchange of gifts there are tears and hugs. Annie tells Ophelia she has never been happier than she is at this very minute, and it is the truth of how she feels. Ophelia would like to say the same to Annie, but she still has the memory of her days with Edward.

It is just after ten when Oliver calls.

"Bring your bicycle," he says.

"But..." Annie stammers. She is going to say not today, but before she can get the words out he hangs up.

Standing there with the receiver still in her hand, she frowns. The request is not all that unusual. She has, on a number of different occasions, brought the bicycle. They often ride into the town square and go for coffee or an ice cream soda, which is all well and good. But today is Christmas, a day for leisurely dining and sitting in front of the fireplace.

Annie is tempted to leave the bicycle at home and simply say she forgot it, but moments before they leave she tosses it into the trunk of the car.

They arrive at Oliver's townhouse shortly before noon. Annie is first out of the car. She lifts the bicycle from the trunk, sits it beside the garage door, then returns to help Ophelia.

The front door is unlocked, as it always is when Oliver knows she is coming. Ophelia is first through the door, but from behind Annie can hear the laughter coming from the living room.

This strikes Annie as strange; Oliver has said nothing about others being there. She and Ophelia follow the sound through the hallway and enter the room. Oliver is standing with his back to the door and doesn't see them enter.

The couple sitting on the opposite side of the room does. The man stands.

"You must be Oliver's someone special," he says and starts toward them.

Oliver turns and gathers both Annie and Ophelia into his arms. He is wearing a smile that stretches the full way across his face.

"Annie, I want you to meet my mom and dad."

Annie gasps. "Ethan Allen? *You're* Ethan Allen?"

Ethan gives a deep hearty laugh. "That I am. Have we met before?"

"Not really," she answers. "But I know of you."

Annie wants to tell him the whole story and perhaps in time she will, but for now there is only a round of introductions and polite getting to know one another.

Laura, Oliver's mother, is soft-spoken and pretty. Ethan is tall, his back straight and shoulders squared. His hair, once brown, is now silver, and his jawline has been softened by time.

At first they talk about inconsequential things: the trip, the weather, Annie's job, Ophelia's garden. Eventually Laura asks how Oliver and Annie met.

Oliver grins. "Annie came here looking for Dad."

"Me?" Ethan Allen asks with a chuckle. "Why me?"

Annie hears the mischievous echo in Ethan's laugh. It is the sound of the boy. She is now able to picture the face that has eluded her for so long.

"I have your bicycle," she says.

Piece by piece the story comes out. Annie tells how she restored the bicycle, but instead of telling how she'd heard his laughter and seen the dog running beside him she simply says it was how she imagined him.

"I could tell by the scratch marks there was once a basket hooked onto the handlebars and figured a boy that age would be running errands for people," she explains.

"What about Dog?" Ethan asks. "How'd you know about Dog?"

"Lucky guess," Annie says with a shrug. "Most boys either want or have a dog."

When Ethan asks where she got the bike and how she knew it was his, Ophelia answers. She sticks to the story Annie has told Oliver, saying it came from one of the Sisters of Mercy.

"Of course, the woman is long gone," Ophelia adds. "So there's no way of knowing where the story originally came from."

One word leads to another, and before long Ethan Allen is telling of his life with Grandma Olivia. When they sit down at the dinner table there is laughter and happiness. Ethan speaks only of the good times and says nothing of the tragedy that came before.

It is not until after they have finished dessert that Annie tells Ethan she has brought the bicycle with her.

"I thought, being it holds such fond memories, you'd like to have it back," she says.

Ethan's face lights up. "You've got it here? Now?"

Annie nods.

"I sure would like to see it again," Ethan says.

They all leave the table and follow Annie out to the driveway where she has left the bike. Ethan spots it the minute they round the walkway.

"Well, I'll be," he says and quickens his step. When he reaches the bike, he throws his leg over the crossbar and takes hold of the handlebars. The memories come flooding back, and his face glows with a recollection of the day he received it.

"Mind if I take it for a spin?" he asks.

"It's yours," Annie says. "Do whatever you want."

Ethan grins and pushes down on the pedal. In less than a second he is off, rolling down the driveway then disappearing down the block.

Annie watches; while others see a man of years on the bike, she sees the boy. It is as she hoped it would be. The memories have gone home.

When Ethan pulls back into the driveway, he knocks the kickstand down and parks the bike.

"I don't think I've ever had a present I enjoyed more."

He wraps his arm around Laura's shoulders and heads for the house. Ophelia and Annie are right behind. Ethan is laughing when he turns to Laura.

"Ah, if that bicycle could talk…the stories it would tell."

It already has, Ophelia thinks, but this thought she keeps to herself.

AS THE YEAR ENDS

Court is recessed for the week between Christmas and New Year's Day, so Oliver's time is his own. Anxious for a few extra hours and the extra pay they will bring, Giselle offers to fill in for Annie so she can enjoy this time with Oliver's parents.

The four of them spend several afternoons together, and little by little Ethan Allen unfolds the tales of his boyhood. He smiles when he speaks of his mama and how she dreamed of going off to New York and singing on the stage of Radio City Music Hall. He tells of the night he came looking for his grandpa but says only that his mama and daddy met an untimely death.

He makes no mention of Scooter Cobb.

When he tells of driving his mama's car with a suitcase behind his back so his legs would reach the pedals, Annie laughs and begs him to tell more. He does, and then one story leads to another and yet another.

The days pass quickly and in what seems barely more than a single afternoon it is the 30th day of December, time for Ethan Allen and Laura to return to Florida. Annie, who has by now grown very fond of Oliver's parents, goes with him when he drives them to the airport.

Once the bags are checked there is a round of hugs, kisses and promises to visit again soon. Then they disappear down the long walkway that leads to their departure gate. When they are gone from sight Annie and Oliver stand by the plate glass window near security, waiting until the plane takes flight. His arm is wrapped around her waist, and her head is leaned onto his broad shoulder.

"Thank you for giving me this," Annie says. "Getting to know your parents was so very special."

"Because of the bicycle?" Oliver asks.

"Partly," she says, "but more so because they're your parents."

Oliver tightens his grip around her waist and tugs her a bit closer.

"They enjoyed meeting you also," he says. "Dad told me he saw something very special in you."

Annie gives a soft chuckle. "I saw something in him too."

What she saw was the boy Ethan Allen once was. What she saw was living proof of the memories she'd glimpsed throughout the long months of searching.

After they leave the airport they drive back to Burnsville and spend a quiet evening with Ophelia. Oliver builds a cozy fire in the parlor, and they gather their chairs around the hearth. Annie brews a pot of dandelion tea, sweetens it with honey and carries the tray with tea and cookies to the parlor.

As they talk Ophelia also says that she enjoyed meeting Ethan Allen and Laura.

"They feel like family," she says but gives no hint as to the future she has seen in her dream. At nine o'clock she yawns and said it is time for such an old woman to be in bed. She kisses Annie's cheek, gives Oliver an affectionate hug then turns toward the staircase.

It is good for young people to have time alone, she thinks. Besides, she is anxious to climb into bed and feel the presence of Edward looking down from the stars.

Now that they are alone, Oliver and Annie move from the chairs and sit beside one another on the sofa. For a while they cuddle together, basking in the warmth of the fire and the closeness of their bodies. There is no awkwardness when he pulls Annie into a passionate embrace. She offers no resistance; it is what she also wants.

He kisses her full on the mouth. After one kiss there is another and another. She wraps her arms around his back and pulls him deeper into the kiss she returns.

When their lips part, he whispers in her ear. "I love you, Annie."

She feels the truth of what he says and returns his words.

"I love you too."

Before the night is out he asks if she will spend New Year's Eve with him.

"I'm planning something special," he says.

There is a moment of hesitation; then Annie explains she is reluctant to leave Ophelia alone on the holiday.

Oliver smiles. He can't be angry, because this thoughtfulness is one of the things he loves about her. He suggests an alternative.

"We can take Ophelia out to an early dinner," he says. "Have an early celebration. Then after she's gone to bed, we can have our own private celebration."

She covers his mouth with a kiss that is answer enough, then whispers, "Perfect."

⌁

Oliver has a dinner reservation at the country club, and when he arrives with Ophelia on one arm and Annie on the other they are escorted back to the table that is waiting. It is just as he has requested: a round table set for three with a ribboned rose on two of the plates. A bottle of champagne is already chilling in the silver bucket that stands beside the table.

As the maître d' pulls the chair out and seats Ophelia, Oliver does so for Annie. He nods, and the champagne glasses are filled. After only a few sips, Ophelia's cheeks are flushed.

"My goodness," she murmurs, "I don't think I have ever been to a New Year's Eve dinner quite this fancy."

"Nothing is too good for my girls," Oliver replies jokingly.

First there is a cup of clear broth with flavors so beautifully blended even Ophelia cannot separate them into ingredients. A hint of rosemary she is certain of, but the others are impossible to name. When they have finished the broth, the waiter brings an artfully crafted salad of endive with a miniature mound of gorgonzola cheese, apple bits and walnuts in the center.

There is no rushing. They eat at a leisurely pace, and Ophelia tells of the first New Year's Eve she and Edward spent in the house.

"That was long before he built the loft," she says. "The only way we could look up and see the first sky of the New Year was to be outside. It was near freezing that night, but we bundled up like Eskimos and took our blanket outside."

She gives a soft smile, and her fondness for the memory is seen in the expression on her face.

For dinner there is a chateaubriand large enough for three. The waiter slices the meat; then, with a set of silver utensils, he spoons the potatoes and vegetables onto each plate and serves it. By the time dessert is placed in front of her, Ophelia has had two glasses of champagne and is starting to yawn. The night is clear and the stars exceptionally bright, so she is anxious to return home and crawl into bed. Edward is certain to be there tonight, and she wants to start the year with him.

It is almost nine-thirty when they arrive back at Memory House. Oliver parks the car in the driveway, and they accompany Ophelia inside. They are barely though the door when she turns toward the staircase.

"I've had a wonderful evening," she says and kisses Oliver on the cheek. Giving him a sly wink she adds, "Now it's time for you two to be off for a celebration of your own."

Annie reaches out and pulls Ophelia into her arms, but before anything more is said Ophelia wrests herself free.

"Be gone," she says, laughing. "Go make some memories of your own."

She knows what Oliver has in mind. He has already spoken to her, and she has given him her blessing.

Happy New Year

After Oliver and Annie have said good night to Ophelia, they
leave Memory House and return to his townhouse in
Wyattsville. In the living room he has the fireplace stacked and
ready to be lit. On the coffee table in front of the sofa there is a tray with
champagne glasses and a dish of chocolates. He snaps on the speakers,
and a pre-programed selection of music begins.

He helps Annie off with her coat then takes her in his arms. He
kisses her mouth then continues with a trail of kisses that runs along her
throat and settles sweetly into the hollow of her collarbone.

The soundtrack of Adele's *One and Only* begins to play and they
dance, their feet barely moving but their bodies swaying together in
perfect unison. The song ends and they step back from one another. What
Oliver feels in his heart is so powerful it is almost hard to hold back, but
still he tries. He wants it to happen at the stroke of midnight. He wants it
to be memorable, something impossible for her to ever forget.

He leaves her in the living room for a moment, goes to the kitchen
and returns with a bottle of champagne. He fills both glasses and
proposes a toast. Annie raises her glass, and when she does so he twines
his arm through hers.

"To a new year and a new life," he says.

As they take the first sip of champagne their arms are locked
together. He hopes it is symbolic of the future.

It is after eleven when the strains of Miley Cyrus's *Adore You* drift
through the speakers. He again pulls her into his arms, and they move to

the music. With his hand pressed tight against her back Oliver whispers the words to the song in her ear.

"I could do this for eternity," he says. "You and me—we're meant to be."

When the song ends Annie offers her mouth to his, and they kiss. It is long and passionate. Annie knows this is more than a moment; it is something that will last a lifetime.

When the grandfather clock chimes the third quarter hour, Oliver knows it is growing close to midnight. He lowers the music, leads Annie over to the sofa and sits beside her. He tells her that he is looking forward to the coming year and all that it will bring.

"I want you to be a part of my life," he says. "Share all that I have and let me love you forever."

Annie looks up and lets her eyes meet his. "There's nothing I would like more."

He brings his lips to hers, and they meet in a long and soulful kiss. When the clock strikes midnight he asks, "Annie Cross, will you marry me?"

Although the kiss has left her nearly breathless, she answers, "Yes!"

For the past several minutes Oliver has been holding a diamond ring in his palm of his hand. He now takes it and slides it onto Annie's finger.

⊙━━◆━━⊙

On the following Sunday a gala brunch is held at Memory House. Giselle and her family are there along with a dozen neighbors who have come to know and love Annie. There is not room enough for everyone to sit, but no one seems to care. This is a festive occasion, and this is all that matters. The guests mingle and move from room to room with small plates of food in one hand and glasses of tea in the other. Some sit on the staircase while others are back to back on the piano bench.

The dining room table is laden with platters of food: thin slices of salmon on triangular toast points, deviled eggs with a sprig of parsley in the center, pieces of ham and cheese on wooden skewers, finger sandwiches, mounds of fresh fruit, petit fours, cookies and three different cakes. In the center of the table is a crystal punch bowl that once belonged to Edward's great aunt Matilda. It is filled with a chilled tea created especially for this occasion.

Ophelia has her silver hair brushed back and curled into a clip. She is wearing the lavender dress that renews the violet color of her eyes. Once her favorite, the dress has been hanging in the back of her closet all but forgotten until now. She is giddy as a schoolgirl, and it is easy to see that Annie's happiness is her happiness also.

Leaning over toward Erma Winston's good ear she whispers, "Oliver is the spitting image of Edward, don't you think?"

Erma peeks across at the man standing next to Annie and nods. She then turns back to Ophelia and says she'll have another glass of the tea.

When Lester Whitley asks if they have set the date yet, Oliver smiles down at Annie and says, "June, perhaps?"

Annie returns his smile and nods.

"Yes, June," she replies. "It's a beautiful time of year for a wedding."

Standing nearby, Ophelia hears this. She has always known the time would come when Annie would leave her house, just as she left her mother's house to begin a life with Edward. This is as it should be, but the thought saddens her.

When the guests have gone and the sky has darkened, Ophelia mounts the stairs, slips into her cotton nightdress and climbs into bed. Before she has settled into herself, she feels the warmth of Edward beside her.

"I was hoping you would come," she says.

She feels the sigh that stirs his soul.

"You know me as well as I know you," he says.

"Love brings people together, and they become as one. You're the other half of me." She hesitates then adds, "It is the same with Annie and Oliver, and for that I am happy."

There is a long moment of silence; then she speaks again.

"My sadness is only because of missing you so."

"Am I not here with you?" he asks. "You have only to search the stars and will always find me. I watch over you as I have always done."

"Yes, and that is a blessing, but it is not the same as being together."

"We will one day be together again, but our time has not yet been written."

"Can you ask for me to be called?"

He chuckles, and it is a sound that warms her heart.

"Such a thing is not possible. You still have much to do on this earth, but when it is written I will come for you."

"When that day comes I will welcome the thought of being together again," she says.

Ophelia closes her eyes and drifts off to sleep. Tonight her dreams will be sweet. They will be dreams of when she and Edward were as Annie and Oliver are now.

THE MEMORY HOUSE SERIES

More about Memory House

If you are reading this, I have to believe you have turned the last page. I hope your visit to Memory House was enjoyable.

In writing this novel, I envisioned it to be a story about stories. Ophelia tells of the memory she discovers in each treasure, but like so many aspects of life there is more. Much more. All of these treasures have a story that came before and after: an unfaithful lover, a lifetime of heartaches, a heavy-handed daddy, a mother who'd give her life to save her child. Each of these stories can be found in one of my other novels.

Spare Change

In *Memory House* Ethan Allen is an old man, but in *Spare Change* he is just a boy—an eleven-year-old lad with a foul mouth and a killer on his tail. He has no one to turn to but a woman who is set in her ways and has no use for children. The bicycle and ball that lead Annie to Oliver are taken from *Spare Change*.

JUBILEE'S JOURNEY

The doll on Ophelia's bed is taken from *Jubilee's Journey* about a child born in the West Virginia mountains and orphaned before she is seven. When she and her older brother go in search of an aunt, he is caught up in a crime not of his making. Jubilee knows the truth, but who is going to believe a seven-year-old child?

PASSING THROUGH PERFECT

The locket is perhaps the saddest of all stories. Taken from *Passing through Perfect*, it belonged to Delia Church. Annie feels the impact of the disaster that came to pass, while Ophelia finds the sweetness of the night Benjamin placed the locket around Delia's neck and swore he'd love her forever.

TWELFTH CHILD

The Lannigan family Bible and the snow globe are both from *The Twelfth Child*. To escape a planned marriage, a willful daughter leaves home and makes her way in a Depression-era world. When she is nearing the tail end of her years, she meets the young woman with whom she forges a friendship that lasts beyond life.

PREVIOUSLY LOVED TREASURES

The watch with all of its memories and dangers belonged to Wilbur Washington, one of the residents of the boarding house in *Previously Loved Treasures*. He would give his life to protect young Caroline and before the night is over, he may have to—unless Peter Pennington's magic is powerful enough to save him.

WISHING FOR WONDERFUL

Ophelia is right when she says the Christmas ornament once held an engagement ring—it happened in *Wishing for Wonderful*. The story, narrated by a Cupid with attitude, will have you laughing out loud as Cupid schemes to give two deserving couples the love they deserve.

WHAT MATTERS MOST

Ophelia is also right about the quilt that covers her bed—it portrays a story of friendship. In *What Matters Most* Louise Palmer is faced with life-altering changes and must choose between friendships and marriage. Although it is at times laugh-out-loud funny, beneath the humor there is a message of love, tolerance and coming to grips with reality.

Last but certainly not least, please know that just as I love holding onto the connection between stories, I love connecting with you, the reader.

I would love to hear what you enjoyed and what you didn't. I'd like to know what you'd like more of, and if you have a story to share I am always willing to listen. The best stories are always the ones that start with a grain of truth and then grow into something magical.

You can contact me through my blog at http://betteleecrosby.com, and while you are there sign up for my newsletter. It's a fun way to stay in touch and every month there's a special giveaway for all of the friends and fans who open the newsletter e-mail to see what's new.

I look forward to seeing you there.

About the Author

AWARD-WINNING NOVELIST BETTE LEE CROSBY brings the wit and wisdom of her Southern Mama to works of fiction—the result is a delightful blend of humor, mystery and romance.

"Storytelling is in my blood," Crosby laughingly admits, "My mom was not a writer, but she was a captivating storyteller, so I find myself using bits and pieces of her voice in most everything I write."

Crosby's work was first recognized in 2006 when she received The National League of American Pen Women Award for a then unpublished manuscript. Since then, she has gone on to win numerous other awards, including The Reviewer's Choice Award, The Reader's Favorite Gold Medal, FPA President's Book Award Gold Medal and The Royal Palm Literary Award.

To learn more about Bette Lee Crosby, explore her other work, or read a sample from any of her books, visit her blog at:

http://betteleecrosby.com

CPSIA information can be obtained
at www.ICGtesting.com
Printed in the USA
LVHW012006300720
661977LV00008BA/1330